'Thanks for you, Rick.

'You convinced everyone at the party that you were my boyfriend.'

They were neighbours, nothing more, she reminded herself. Rick wasn't looking for a meaningful relationship. And she certainly didn't want to become involved with another man hot on the heels of her disastrous engagement. So why did she feel such an intense longing to throw herself into his arms?

His voice cut into her thoughts. 'It's a pity that I can only lend myself out for this all too brief evening,' he said carefully. 'You know that's how it's got to be, don't you, Maddy?' His eyes were fixed intently on hers. 'My job doesn't leave much space for romantic relationships.'

She closed her eyes and tried to banish the memory of dancing in his arms. 'I totally understand that you want to be a professional bachelor, Rick.' Silence filled the space around them.

'That was my plan,' he muttered, eventually.

Barbara Hannay was born in Sydney, educated in Brisbane and has spent most of her adult life living in tropical North Queensland, where she and her husband have raised four children. While she has enjoyed many happy times camping and canoeing in the bush, she also delights in an urban lifestyle—chamber music, contemporary dance, movies and dining out. An English teacher, she has always loved writing, and now, by having her stories published, she is living her most cherished fantasy.

Recent titles by the same author:

OUTBACK WIFE AND MOTHER
THE WEDDING COUNTDOWN

BORROWED BACHELOR

BY
BARBARA HANNAY

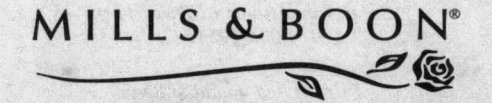

MILLS & BOON®

DID YOU PURCHASE THIS BOOK WITHOUT A COVER?

If you did, you should be aware it is **stolen property** as it was reported *unsold and destroyed* by a retailer. Neither the author nor the publisher has received any payment for this book.

All the characters in this book have no existence outside the imagination of the author, and have no relation whatsoever to anyone bearing the same name or names. They are not even distantly inspired by any individual known or unknown to the author, and all the incidents are pure invention.

All Rights Reserved including the right of reproduction in whole or in part in any form. This edition is published by arrangement with Harlequin Enterprises II B.V. The text of this publication or any part thereof may not be reproduced or transmitted in any form or by any means, electronic or mechanical, including photocopying, recording, storage in an information retrieval system, or otherwise, without the written permission of the publisher.

This book is sold subject to the condition that it shall not, by way of trade or otherwise, be lent, resold, hired out or otherwise circulated without the prior consent of the publisher in any form of binding or cover other than that in which it is published and without a similar condition including this condition being imposed on the subsequent purchaser.

MILLS & BOON and MILLS & BOON with the Rose Device are registered trademarks of the publisher.

*First published in Great Britain 1999
Harlequin Mills & Boon Limited,
Eton House, 18-24 Paradise Road, Richmond, Surrey TW9 1SR*

© Barbara Hannay 1999

ISBN 0 263 81939 6

*Set in Times Roman 10½ on 12 pt.
02-0002-49542 C1*

*Printed and bound in Spain
by Litografia Rosés, S.A., Barcelona*

CHAPTER ONE

SHE only needed to reach just a little higher.

Maddy Delancy tested her weight as she balanced on the top of the stepladder. So far so good. If she rose onto her tiptoes, she should be able to attach the cane basket brimming with greenery to the hook in the ceiling and then her shop's window display would be complete.

It was touch-and-go for a moment. The stepladder wobbled within the same split second that Maddy caught a glimpse, out of the corner of her eye, of a man's alarmed face through the window. Crazy visions of falling flashed into her mind—of the ladder toppling—even smashing through the pane of glass and taking her with it.

But, to her immense relief, the stepladder righted without mishap. The chain holding the hanging basket slipped over the hook with a satisfying clunk and Maddy was able to climb back down in time to see the man, who'd been staring at her, rush through her rose-festooned doorway and almost skid to a halt just in front of her.

She had the distinct impression that this tall, dark male was dashing to her rescue and she found the thought charming. Perhaps if the stepladder had wobbled some more, fate might have had her falling into his arms, and she'd be clinging to him now, her eyes shining with eternal gratitude.

Worse things could happen. The fellow had all the hallmarks of a knight in shining armour. His height, broad shoulders, thick, dark brown hair, not to mention his ruggedly handsome face, were all features which, for her money, fitted quite well into the perfect hero image. And, she realised with growing interest, this was the same man she'd seen this morning moving his things into the flat upstairs.

Maddy wondered if it was time to lift her self-imposed ban prohibiting all interest in the opposite sex. Six weeks ago, her fiancé, Byron, had suddenly broken off their engagement with all the delicacy and finesse of an erupting volcano.

She had done her best to put Byron out of her mind. The first step had been to move her bank account to a different branch, so she wouldn't have to run across him at his work. But her chest still thumped painfully whenever she caught sight of a handsome, fair-headed man of medium height dressed in a grey business suit. And even now, whenever she thought of Byron it would take ages for her heart to subside to its accustomed rhythmic beat and for her breathing to steady.

The whole experience had been so devastating, she'd sworn off men for ever.

So, this morning, she was quite surprised to find herself surreptitiously checking that her pale pink blouse was still neatly tucked into her jeans as she flashed the newcomer a bright smile. 'Hello there, may I help you?'

'Help *me*?' he asked, looking puzzled, and his uncertainty cemented her first impression that he'd rushed into her shop thinking she was about to fall. But she had to admire the speed with which his expression switched from confusion to defiant confidence.

'You wanted some flowers?' she suggested.

'Yes, of course.' His steel-grey eyes swept the shop's interior, taking in the buckets of fresh flowers clustered on the floor, the dried arrangements of vivid wild flowers lining the shelves on the far wall and the two glass-fronted refrigerators holding more floral decorations. 'I—I'm visiting someone in hospital.'

She gestured to the buckets at their feet. 'Did you want something fresh?'

He ran lean fingers through his rain-spattered hair while he scanned the colourful array. Roses, orchids, carnations—pink, mauve, white. As Maddy waited patiently, she pushed wispy dark curls away from her face. 'These Love Potion and Angel Face roses are on special.'

He slanted her a reproachful smile. 'You can spare me the sales pitch. My friend's not the roses type.'

'Then perhaps these blue irises?' With her sneaker-enclosed foot she pointed to a bucket holding one lone bunch of striking blue flowers with yellow throats.

'Yes. They're nearer the mark. They'll be fine, thanks.' He smiled again. This time it was a stunning smile that not only warmed his grey eyes, but brought heat to her cheeks.

And as she bent down to lift the irises from the water Maddy was aware of his curious gaze appraising her. But he looked away quickly as she straightened and he concentrated his attention on the shop's bright pink and purple sign. Bordered by flowers, it stood out against the stark white of the painted brick wall. *Floral Fantasies...we aim for the heart.*

'Clever slogan.' His head jerked in the direction of the sign.

'Thanks.' In response to his meagre show of interest she plucked up the courage to add, 'You've just moved in upstairs, haven't you? I saw you this morning, carting up your gear.' Holding out her hand, she smiled, 'I'm

Madeline Delancy. We're neighbours. I have a little flat behind the shop.'

He seemed taken aback by her sudden friendliness. Maybe she was acting a little over-eager. Nevertheless, he shook her hand and grunted, 'Rick Lawson.'

'My friends—*most* people—call me Maddy,' she added, and looked at him expectantly.

'Maddy?' For the briefest moment, his eyes gleamed, but Maddy couldn't be sure whether the spark was stirred by irritation or interest.

'You're lucky,' she said, determined not to be put off by his reticence. She shook water away from the stems. 'This is my last bunch.'

He made no response as he followed her to the counter and with deft, sure movements she wrapped clear Cellophane dotted with jaunty yellow spots around the bouquet. 'That should cheer the patient up! I've pinned the Cellophane over at the top to keep the rain out.'

As she handed him the flowers, a figure huddled inside a shiny red raincoat dashed into the shop, spilling raindrops.

'Maddy! You're just the person I need.'

Maddy recognised the woman with bright blonde hair and felt her smile vanish with the speed of a light switch being flicked on. 'Cynthia? I—I haven't seen you for ages.'

And haven't missed you one jot, she would have liked to add. Cynthia Graham was one of her least favourite people.

Cynthia didn't respond. Her heavily made-up eyes were scanning the fresh flowers frantically. 'Oh, no! There are none here!' she wailed, and shot a startled look at Maddy. 'Don't you have any blue irises?'

Her annoyed glance swept over Rick, taking in the

wallet he'd just extracted from his hip pocket and the bunch of irises he gripped in his other hand. Her eyebrows rose in consternation. 'Have you bought them? Have you taken the last bunch?'

'I'm sorry, Cynthia,' Maddy interrupted quickly. 'Just as soon as I've attended to this gentleman, I'm sure I will be able to help you find something else suitable.'

She was aware of Rick Lawson's gaze darting from one female to the other.

'But I wanted them for Byron,' Cynthia explained impatiently.

'Byron?'

This time it wasn't just the smile that left Maddy's face. She felt a cold sweat break out and her shoulders slumped. What on earth did her ex-fiancé have to do with Cynthia? An ice-cold sense of premonition swamped her and she clutched the counter for support.

But even as her mind floundered she sensed that Rick Lawson was getting edgy, standing impatiently waiting to pay for his flowers while this tense exchange took place. She cleared her throat in an attempt to finish serving him when Cynthia interrupted.

'Maddy, didn't you know about Byron and me?' Her crooning voice was loaded with pseudo-concern and insincerity and she cast a sly glance over her shoulder to Rick, before continuing. 'I hate to be the one to tell you this, sweetie, especially when you were so sure you were going to marry the dear boy, but since he broke off with you—well, I'm afraid he's fallen madly in love with me.'

'He's what?' A thick, painful sob rose in Maddy's throat.

'Byron and I are engaged.'

Lifting a shaking hand to her mouth, Maddy tried to

ward off a hollow wave of nausea. She felt giddy. And so embarrassed to have a stranger like Rick Lawson overhearing Cynthia's shocking news!

He'd feigned disinterest by turning his back on them and, with arms folded across his chest, he was staring at something on the ceiling.

Somehow, the sight of that broad, resentful back urged Maddy to pull herself together, but it took every atom of her willpower. 'I'm so happy that you're happy, Cynthia,' she chirped, in what she hoped sounded like a spontaneous response. Then she added defiantly, 'But don't worry about me. I'm well set up now.'

Cynthia's fair eyebrow arched in disbelief and Maddy's hands clenched. Flustered, she rushed on. 'I have a new boyfriend.' She nodded quickly towards Rick's turned back. 'He's just moving in today.' The enormous lie doubled the pace of Maddy's heartbeats.

Cynthia's face pulled into an expression of grudging approval mingled with self-centred disappointment. Maddy couldn't have hoped for a better reaction.

But Rick had clearly had enough. With a burst of annoyance, he turned, scowling, shoved his wallet back into the pocket of his jeans and dropped the bunch of irises back on the counter. 'Here, you buy them,' he growled at Cynthia. 'I can get them another day. My friend's going to be in hospital for a long time.'

Maddy struggled frantically to think clearly. 'Are you sure? You don't have to…'

'No, look, really,' Rick demurred, raising his hands to ward off any protests and backing towards the shop door. It was clear he wanted to get out of the place. 'It really isn't a big deal.' He flashed them both a teeth-gritted version of a smile before striding quickly out of the shop.

'It's very kind of you,' Maddy called after him.

As he disappeared, Cynthia's eyes narrowed. 'You can easily get him some more if he's about to move in with you, can't you?' she asked.

Maddy looked at her blankly. Then she blushed. 'Yes. Yes, of course I can. It's not a problem. Give my regards to Byron.'

And she held herself together until Cynthia walked out of the shop door clutching her irises. But as soon as the other woman had gone she snatched up the empty bucket that had held the flowers and stomped to the little room at the back of the shop where she thumped it down with a loud crash.

Damn Cynthia! Double damn Byron!

After six weeks, she'd thought the scars were finally healing. But now... Byron engaged again? To Cynthia Graham? How could he?

How could *she*?

But Maddy knew the answer to that. Cynthia Graham had been an old rival since high school. Anything Maddy could do, scheming Cynthia would always do better, if it killed her...

It was a pattern so old, Maddy knew she shouldn't be surprised that it had been repeated once again. Cynthia Graham had always wanted everything she ever wanted, whether it was getting into the netball team, or winning an art prize. And later she managed to date just about any boy Maddy ever went out with. She should have known Cynthia would chase after Byron.

And now look at the mess she'd made of things. She'd panicked and become so desperately flustered that she'd let Cynthia think Rick Lawson was her boyfriend. Thank heavens he had no idea. There was already a woman in his life he cared deeply enough about to want to buy her flowers.

That was another thing. This friend of Rick Lawson's was sick in hospital and surely she deserved those flowers much more than *Byron*!

She could picture Rick visiting his friend. He would present her with the bright bouquet—bending low to her hospital bed to give her a kiss. It would be a touching scene. He was so very nice-looking—especially when he smiled. And she could imagine how pleased the patient would be to see him.

Maddy tried to pinpoint where she'd seen Rick before. There was something strangely familiar about his face *and* his name. Early this morning, he'd made several trips past her window carting up his luggage through the rain. But bulging backpacks and high-tech camera equipment seemed to be the sum total of his belongings.

She shrugged as she reached for the phone while running her finger down the list of other florist outlets taped to the wall beside her small desk. Whoever he was, he had dashed into her shop like a man on a desperate mission. He'd taken great pains to select exactly the right flowers. And then he'd gallantly surrendered them to Cynthia, as if they hadn't mattered at all.

Maddy stared through the small window in the shop's back wall. The rain, so unseasonal for sunny Brisbane, was still streaming down outside. She didn't really fancy heading out into such miserable weather, but the least she could do was find Rick Lawson a replacement bunch.

At six-thirty, Maddy rapped a confident knock on her new neighbour's door and summoned her brightest smile as it opened. But her smile wavered as she encountered grey eyes regarding her warily, as if she were casing the joint, or at the very least trying to sell something.

When Maddy thrust a bunch of irises forward, Rick merely frowned. 'Good evening,' she began, trying not to sound too hesitant. 'I managed to get some more irises and I thought I'd deliver them as soon as possible in case you were going back to the hospital tonight.'

'Thanks,' he muttered as he accepted the bouquet. Maddy felt her eyes widen. He wasn't exactly rude, but there was certainly something exceedingly guarded about his expression.

'It was no trouble,' she offered. 'The Golden Wattle in Adelaide Street had plenty of these flowers to spare and…seeing we're neighbours…' Her voice trailed off uncertainly.

Rick was staring at the bunch of flowers, a deep frown drawing his brows low.

'I'm very sorry about the tussle over the flowers this afternoon.' Maddy tried again. 'I hope your…um…the patient—I hope she wasn't too disappointed.'

'Sam?' The tanned skin around the grey eyes crinkled and Maddy thought she caught a hint of a smile. 'It wasn't a problem.'

She bit her lip uncertainly. Why was this stranger making her feel so inadequate? She had always considered herself to be very good with people. While her successful business had always depended on her skills in public relations, she'd gone out of her way to be on friendly terms with her neighbours as well. Life was much more comfortable that way.

She tossed her long dark curls over her shoulder and waited in the vain hope that he would be more forthcoming. Perhaps he would tell her about the woman in hospital. Anything to be sociable. But Rick Lawson clearly didn't feel the need to make any kind of small talk.

She shrugged. If her new neighbour had the social skills of a newt, it was a pity, but she'd get over it. 'Look.' She tried one last time. 'I know you've just moved in here. I don't mean to pry or anything. I just wanted to apologise about the flowers and perhaps I could—I don't know—maybe I could cook you a meal some time as a kind of compensation. While you're settling in,' she added with her most encouraging smile— the one she used for uncertain customers. 'I mean if you're spending a lot of time at the hospital, you might be pretty tied up...and I'm always cooking extra food for my kid brother at uni. He claims they starve him.'

'That won't be necessary.'

His bluntness angered her. Maddy stiffened. Why couldn't this man be a little more grateful? Helping him would be a useful distraction. It would help *her* forget her other woes and she would feel less guilty about using him as a weapon against Cynthia. 'You're going to be obstinate, aren't you?' she challenged him.

'Good Lord, woman!' Rick exclaimed, with an exaggerated heave of his shoulders. 'I'm saving you from having to cook dinner for me. How does that make me obstinate?'

She shook her curls defensively. 'This afternoon you seemed terribly anxious to buy some flowers for your friend. The next minute Cynthia Graham virtually grabbed them off you for—for the stupidest of reasons. I felt bad—especially as you're not just any customer. You're my neighbour. I like to get on with my neighbours and—and I'd like to be able to compensate.'

Rick shoved his free hand deep into the pocket of his track pants and an eyebrow arched. 'Ms Delancy,' he said with exaggerated forbearance, 'how about we agree that I shall put in a compensation claim if and when I feel you or your business have inconvenienced me in any way? Does that sound acceptable?'

It sounded to Maddy like a pretty clear snub. She could add it to her list of recent failures. It was bad enough that Byron had dumped her in preference for Cynthia. But now even this mature-age street kid was shunning her friendly overtures. Perhaps he had her tagged as a loser?

'It doesn't sound like good neighbourly relations,' she said huffily.

'For Pete's sake,' Rick Lawson cried, running distracted fingers through his hair. 'This isn't the United Nations. We are simply a man and a woman who happen to live in the same building. We don't need *any* kind of a relationship. You just concentrate on this new fellow who's moving in with you.'

Maddy stared at him, her mouth opening and closing while she tried to think of *anything* to say.

Rick took advantage of her dilemma to drive his point home. 'Look, I know you've had some kind of bust-up with your fiancé. But it's got nothing to do with me. I'm not a counsellor. Sorting out your love life is a job for your new boyfriend.'

Her face was bright red. She could feel it. This morning in the shop he'd heard every word of her reply to Cynthia. It was small comfort that he hadn't actually seen her indicating that *he* was the boyfriend in question. Maddy had never felt so embarrassed, so caught out, so angry!

Lifting her head as proudly as she could, she glared at him. 'My love life is fine, thank you. You must have a warped view of the world if you interpret every friendly gesture as related to—to sex!'

With another toss of her head, she spun around in a rather poor imitation of a pirouette. Unfortunately, she finished awkwardly and staggered for the first few steps as she tried to march haughtily away. But at least Rick Lawson had the good grace not to chuckle—not so loudly that she heard it at any rate.

During the week that followed, the monster upstairs made Maddy cringe or feel angry every time she saw him. He passed her shop several times each day, starting with an early morning jog around the time she arrived back from the markets. So she was provided with far too many opportunities to seesaw between self-recrimination for making such a mess of a simple friendly gesture and self-righteous wrath whenever she remembered his biting responses. How had she ever thought of him as some kind of *hero*?

They'd virtually ignored each other all week. A curt 'good morning' or an unsmiling nod was the most they'd exchanged.

But by Friday evening Maddy had begun to put the silly episode behind her. Mr Lawson certainly wasn't worth another moment's mental anguish. She tried not to let it bother her that he'd probably guessed by now that there was no new boyfriend.

At seven o'clock she closed her timber venetian blinds to block out the lights of Inner Brisbane and with her stereo system playing the hushed, slow crooning of her favourite jazz CD she curled contentedly on her sofa.

A plate of toast piled with beans and a mug of hot mocha sat on the coffee table beside her and a whole weekend stretched in front of her. Blissfully she crunched into a piece of toast topped with spicy beans and contemplated what her weekend held.

Chrissie, her part-time assistant, looked after the shop on Saturday mornings, so all Maddy had to concentrate on was the flowers for the Jameson wedding in the afternoon. And that was more or less in hand. Sunday would be hers.

But, socially...it was an empty weekend with no dates, no invitations.

Of course, no Byron.

Maddy tried to shrug away the thought. She couldn't afford to let her mind wander down that weary, worn-out track. Thinking about Byron with Cynthia was even more hurtful and distressing than contemplating Rick Lawson.

When her doorbell rang, she remained quite calm. After weeks of leaping to answer the telephone's ring or a knock on the door, Maddy at last knew, without any shadow of a doubt, that there was no chance the caller would be Byron. Slowly she rose to her feet and dusted toast crumbs from her T-shirt. As she padded across the room in her bare feet, Maddy noticed a bean had rolled down her front, leaving a bright amber trail over one breast, so she dabbed at the stain with a tissue. But the orange glob simply spread further.

She swung the door open and took two rapid steps back.

'Hi,' said Rick Lawson.

'Oh!' Her mouth stayed open in a silly, round circle.

The sight of him dressed casually in jeans and a black polo shirt and filling her doorway with his one hundred percent all-male presence stunned her. What on earth was he doing here?

'Mr Lawson?' After her week of pent-up resentment,

she could only think of one reason why he would be calling. 'Have you come to apologise?'

His brows shot down into a deep V. 'Pardon?'

Maddy felt her eyes roll towards the ceiling. 'You realise you were rude to me last week after I went to a lot of trouble to get you those flowers.'

He stepped forward into her flat and Maddy found herself taking another step back.

'I wasn't being rude, Madeline. Just cautious.'

'And I'm being cautious now. What do you want?' she asked.

'I need some advice.'

'Really?'

'Really,' he replied with an amused smile. 'After considering your little lecture on good neighbourly relations, I've decided to accept your offer.'

'My offer?' she echoed, at the same time flinching at the inanity of her question. Surely she wasn't going to flounder through another moronic episode of foot-and-mouth disease?

'Dinner,' he replied with annoying succinctness. From behind his back he produced a bottle of expensive-looking red wine.

'But you refused that offer,' she protested, hands on hips.

Rick cocked his head to one side and rubbed his chin thoughtfully. Then he grinned. Maddy noticed rather irrelevantly that he had nice teeth. 'I need a change of scenery. Sam's feeling much better and getting stroppy. And I think you might be able to help me.'

'I don't see how I can help you, Rick,' Maddy countered, feeling totally confused. 'I'm quite sure you don't need my advice on how to humour your friend while she recuperates.'

Rick chuckled. He handed Maddy the wine and she accepted it, but stood there holding it in front of her while she waited for an explanation. He scratched his head. 'I'm interested in some business advice. You seem to have a pretty good little outfit running here. And I'm keen to do some networking on my partner's behalf.'

Maddy felt her lips flatten into a half-hearted smile. She'd only inherited her grandfather's shop eighteen months ago and didn't consider herself all that experienced. And she was hardly flattered that Rick Lawson considered her company an improvement on the grumpy Sam. But then again, on a lonely Friday evening, anything that helped her forget about Byron was a bonus.

Rick strode across her lounge room towards the kitchen, and he sniffed as he walked. 'What are you eating? Can I smell chilli?'

'Chilli beans,' she answered without enthusiasm. 'On toast.' He *would* pick the one night she was having a scratch meal!

'With cheese?'

She almost responded in her usual manner by jumping straight into hostess mode. Maddy was more than capable of hauling a range of items out of her well-stocked fridge and throwing together quite a presentable meal. But, she reminded herself, this was Rick Lawson, the moody and undeserving monster from upstairs. There was nothing to be gained by bending over backwards to impress him.

'No cheese,' she lied airily.

'Salsa?'

'No.'

'I suppose corn chips or sour cream would be out of the question?'

'Completely.'

He pivoted, then stood with feet firmly planted on her hand-woven rug, and his mouth pulled into a rueful smile. His eyes shimmered as he hooked his thumbs through the loops of his jeans and Maddy couldn't help noticing the snug fit of blue denim over well-toned, masculine muscles.

'I wasn't expecting you,' she said.

'Of course you weren't,' Rick replied with a shrug. 'Will your boyfriend mind?'

Maddy's stomach plummeted. She shook her head. If she were brave, she would confess now that there was no boyfriend—that she'd only invented him in an attempt to ward off Cynthia's oppressive one-upmanship.

But she wasn't brave.

'He—he's not home tonight,' she stammered. 'He—he's taking evening classes and he had to go to a lecture.'

Rick's eyes widened. 'And he won't mind if you dine with a stranger?'

'Oh, of course not!' she spluttered. 'He's not the jealous type and—and anyhow, you're my—our neighbour, hardly a stranger.' Thoroughly flustered now, she flounced past him into the kitchen. 'I'll see how much is left in the pot.'

He followed her. 'Even though it's smaller, your place looks a lot classier than mine.' Rick's gaze scanned Maddy's flat with interest, taking in the glowing timber floors and blinds and the deep royal-blue walls, which provided a striking backdrop for her collection of bright prints. 'I have an old, moth-eaten carpet in a delightful shade of baby-poop yellow and a slightly lighter version of the same fetching hue on the walls.'

Maddy handed him back the wine bottle plus a corkscrew then took a step back. In her tiny kitchen, he suddenly seemed bigger, even more overwhelmingly male. 'Interior decorating is my hobby,' she said as she scraped beans away from the sides of a saucepan, sloshed in a dollop of chilli sauce and placed it back on a low heat. 'I get urges to make any place I live in as comfortable and cheery as possible, so I talked the landlord into letting me do up these rooms. He provided the materials, I supplied the elbow grease.' She dropped two slices of bread into her toaster.

'You've done a great job,' Rick admitted as he pulled the cork out of the bottle. It came with a gentle pop. His lazy smile mocked her. 'So you have an overdeveloped nesting instinct?'

Maddy sniffed. 'What's so funny? I put a lot of energy into my business, but my home is important to me as well.'

'Sounds smart.' He lifted a restraining hand. 'There's no need to wave that wooden spoon at me like that. Your shirt already has a bad case of the measles.'

She looked down at her white T-shirt. A splattering of bright red dots had joined the stain she'd noticed earlier. But, worse than a little mess, she noticed that, under Rick Lawson's sardonic gaze, her nipples were hardening into obvious tight buds, straining against the thin cotton fabric. She dumped the spoon back in the pot and, as casually as possible, crossed her arms over her chest.

The toast popped up and Maddy was grateful for the diversion. She placed the slices on a plate and spooned beans onto them. 'You'll find a knife and fork in that drawer to your left. And wineglasses in the cupboard above.'

As she carried their food to the glass-topped table at one end of the lounge-dining room while Rick followed with the wine and glasses, Maddy reprimanded herself for being so easily manipulated. Rick had arrived uninvited and totally spoiled her peaceful evening. And somehow she'd let him get away with it.

'I guess you do a lot of business for people visiting the hospital,' he said as he filled her wineglass.

So he really does want to discuss my business, she realised, faintly surprised. 'There are florists right at the hospital door who do a roaring trade there. My sales are more of a mixture.'

Rick took a deep swig of his wine. 'Weddings, celebrations? Do you have much work in that line?' His tone sounded deliberately casual.

Maddy toyed with her glass. Where was this leading to? Was he from some big chain wanting to take over her business? The thought chilled her. She loved her little shop and the thought of losing it was unbearable. But surely she was letting her imagination get the better of her. 'I'm moderately successful in that area,' she said, and decided to leave it at that.

Rick sampled the beans and nodded his approval as he chewed. 'Tasty,' he commented. 'Beans go quite well with the wine, don't they?'

Maddy's hand waggled vaguely in the air. The beans were average as chilli beans went, but the wine was very good quality. 'This wine would improve just about anything—even a peanut butter sandwich.' She took another sip to prove it. 'I'm glad to hear your partner is getting better.'

'Yeah. It's going to be a long process, but mobility should be retained.'

'So she's had an accident?'

For a long moment, Rick stared back at her, and she was shocked by the sudden change in his expression.

His grey eyes became as empty and bleak as the ashen shell of a burnt-out building.

'A bullet lodged in the hip.'

'My God!'

Rick frowned and blinked and stared at his food, and Maddy lowered her eyes to her own plate. Her thoughts whirled.

Rick Lawson's girlfriend had been shot?

Who was she sharing her meal with?

A criminal involved in some kind of backstreet warfare?

She thought of Rick's few belongings. Was he on the run? The hairs lifted on the back of her neck as she remembered how familiar his face and name had seemed. Surely she hadn't seen mugshots of him on television? On some 'Wanted' file?

'I blame myself,' Rick said with a heavy sigh. And the expression on his face was so full of remorse that Maddy put on hold her intention to ring Crime Stoppers. Surely a criminal wouldn't look so repentant?

'Perhaps you're being too hard on yourself,' she said, shocked at the definite note of sympathy she heard in her voice.

Rick's eyes softened and he smiled a slow, lingering smile that acknowledged her attempt at empathy, but held just a hint of something else as well.

As his gaze rested on her, Maddy's arms turned to goosebumps and her cheeks grew warm. What was wrong with her? She knew better than to feel warm and melting over a man's smile. Especially a man who already had a girlfriend. So what if the smile was a darn sight beyond charming? So what if his eyes suddenly sparked with a hint of something that looked remarkably like desire? And perhaps his mouth was sensuous and sexy? Minutes—maybe only seconds ago, she'd been suspecting this man of being wanted by the police in at least five states.

But, whatever message had flashed across his face, it disappeared as he shook his head. 'Sam's accident was my fault. It was my idea for us to chase a story in a really dangerous part of the world.'

Rick placed his wineglass carefully on the glass-topped table. 'Sam didn't want to do the story. Said the whole situation was too hazardous. But such a damned good photographer can't resist a chance at good footage—and I knew that once we got there and saw the action Sam would be right in the thick of things—getting the most incredible scenes.' He paused and, with his fork, traced a pattern in the bright sauce on his plate. 'I placed my partner's life in jeopardy for the sake of my story.'

While her sympathy for him swelled, something else clicked into place in Maddy's brain. 'I just realised who you are,' she blurted out.

CHAPTER TWO

'YOU'RE Rick Lawson!' Maddy exclaimed.

He grinned briefly and rolled his eyes. 'Well done,' he chuckled. 'I thought I introduced myself last Monday.'

'No. I mean you're *the* Rick Lawson. The foreign correspondent!'

How could she not have recognised him? On her father's recommendation, Maddy had watched Rick's programs from around the world with increasing fascination. She'd been impressed by his ability to make complicated and often disastrous situations in foreign parts of the world seem clear and vitally important to viewers watching from the comfort of their lounge rooms.

But, meeting him in a totally different context—in her own little flower shop—she hadn't made the connection. As soon as he'd mentioned terms like stories and photographers, his identity had been so glaringly obvious, she felt foolish. 'Wow! You did all that wonderful work for famine relief last year!' she exclaimed.

'And landed my partner in hospital this year,' he replied softly.

'But you said she's going to get better.'

'Sam will walk again. But there'll probably be a limp. We won't be able to do the dangerous kind of work we're used to doing together.'

Rick reached over and topped up her glass and promptly changed the subject. 'The people like you whose business involves weddings—the caterers, florists, photographers... Do you all form some kind of a cooperative? Recommend each other? That sort of thing?'

'Oh—um—are you planning a wedding?' Maddy stammered, still grappling with the startling realisation that, rather than harbouring a criminal, she was entertaining a celebrity.

'No, not at all. But I thought maybe Sam should think about that line of work—some kind of functions photographer. Videos perhaps.'

'Oh. I see,' Maddy said quietly.

And she saw a lot more. It suddenly made complete sense why the taciturn Rick Lawson, who'd shunned her all week, had suddenly turned up on her doorstep. He was no more interested in 'good neighbourly relations' now than he had been on Monday.

That winning smile he'd beamed on her mere minutes ago had been a weapon—a weapon he frequently used in front of the camera. He could switch it on whenever he needed to win the hearts of viewers worldwide. And tonight he'd turned it on for her, because he wanted to appease his guilty conscience by finding a suitable career alternative for his partner. He was simply sussing her out as a possible link for Sam's future employment.

And why she should be so utterly disappointed by that thought puzzled Maddy totally.

Rick stood up. 'Why don't you have the last of this wine while I wash the dishes?'

Startled, Maddy jumped to her feet. She hadn't expected Rick Lawson to belong to the dish-washing variety of male. She'd hardly met a man who had. At home, her father had always had more important things to do than household chores and her brothers had helped him on the farm, leaving the kitchen to her mother and herself. More recently, while her fiancé had enjoyed her cooking on many occasions, she knew Byron would have had a blue fit if she'd so much as waved a tea towel at him.

'You don't need to wash up,' she told Rick. 'There are only a couple of plates and a pot.'

But he ignored her protests, gathered up the plates and headed for the kitchen. 'I insist.'

Maddy followed him, clutching her wineglass. She leant against a cupboard and watched with interest as Rick flicked on the hot-water tap and squeezed some detergent into the sink. She had to admit that her interest was fuelled by more than simple curiosity about a man tackling a household chore. The muscles flexing in Rick's shoulders and arms as he moved, the way detergent bubbles clung to the light hair on his strong forearms and the neat way his jeans outlined his behind were all points worthy of inspection.

She set down her drink, reached for a tea towel and furiously scrubbed at a plate. There was no point in wasting time contemplating Rick Lawson's physique when the only interest he'd shown in her was as an employment agency for his girlfriend.

'Do you have a pot-scrubber?' he asked as he frowned at the baked-on dregs of beans sticking to the bottom of the saucepan.

'Sure,' Maddy mumbled, feeling ridiculously flustered and frantic. It was so weird to be sharing a domestic chore with a virtual stranger. 'Under the sink. I'll get it for you.'

He stepped slightly to one side so that she could rummage around in the cupboard. How could the scouring gear have vanished? It was always in a little plastic bucket at the front of the cupboard. On her haunches, she stuck her head deeper into the rather untidy jumble of cleaning gear.

At last she saw the scourer right at the back of the cupboard. As she reached for it, her phone chose to ring and Maddy automatically straightened. Her head hit the drainpipe. 'Ouch!' she wailed as she staggered backwards and fell against Rick's legs.

'Whoa,' he chuckled, and his wet, soapy hands grasped her shoulders. 'Are you OK?'

Maddy nodded and he helped her up while the phone continued its insistent ringing. 'I should get that,' she muttered. But she was too late. As she headed across the kitchen, her answering machine cut in and her caller's voice was broadcast through the small flat.

'Hello, Madeline. Surprise, surprise. It's Byron.'

Maddy froze mid-step. Her heart thumped frantically and her chest tightened as if her childhood asthma had returned. She wanted to run to the phone and snatch it up, but her feet wouldn't carry her quickly. She staggered across the kitchen as if she were fighting her way through dense forest. Byron? What on earth did he want?

She didn't want to know.

But his message continued, his voice sounding a little thinner than she remembered. 'I understand Cynthia has told you our news, Maddy. About our engagement. We'd really love you to do all the flowers for our wedding. Please give us a call. Same number. Bye.'

How long she stood there, staring at the answering machine, her hands clasped as if in prayer while her heart galloped a chaotic route around her rib cage, she couldn't tell.

A discreet cough disturbed her wretched thoughts. Rick stood beside her.

'You're finished?' she whispered.

'I could well ask you the same question,' he replied. 'You look as if you've been totally finished—done in, done over. I take it that wasn't good news?'

'No.' She tried to smile but somehow the muscles around her mouth wouldn't cooperate. 'It was—I mean—it—it's just another job.'

'Of course it isn't *just* another job,' he said, his voice all deep and gravelly. 'You're a really shocking shade of pale. You look like you've just had a close encounter with a vampire.'

She stared at him for a long moment. 'In a way I have,' she whispered, the aftershock of Byron's bombshell still sending sickening waves shooting through her.

He guided her towards the sofa. 'You need to sit down.'

Maddy slumped onto the sofa and Rick sat beside her, watching her carefully. 'You don't have to tell me about the vampire if you don't want to,' he said. 'You should probably save it for your boyfriend. What time does he get back?'

'Oh—um—not till late,' she mumbled. She managed a weak smile. 'Don't worry about me, Rick. I know you don't want to get embroiled in my personal problems.'

Rick eyed her shrewdly. 'There's no such animal, is there?'

'What?'

'This boyfriend. I'm no Sherlock Holmes, but there's absolutely no evidence of a bloke in this flat. If he does exist, he must be the neatest fellow who ever walked this planet—and be very clever at slipping in and out of this place when no one's around. I haven't seen hide nor hair of him in a week.'

Maddy plucked at a loose thread in the fabric on her

sofa. There was absolutely no point in trying to cover up any longer. 'No,' she sighed. 'There's no new boyfriend.' Then she hastily added, 'At the moment.'

'You just wanted to shut up that woman in the shop the other day,' Rick conceded. 'She was one nasty piece of work.'

Maddy could have kissed Rick. It felt so good to realise he understood. He had read Cynthia like a book. 'It was all I could think of on the spur of the moment,' she admitted.

With lazy nonchalance, Rick settled himself lower on the sofa. 'This Byron fellow who rang tonight is your ex-fiancé. Right?'

Maddy nodded. 'He—well, he called our engagement off just six weeks ago. And now—he's engaged again!' As a fresh wave of anger surfaced, Maddy clenched her fists. 'And he has the gall to ring up and ask me to do the flowers for his—for crying out loud—his new wedding! But the worst thing is, he's marrying *Cynthia Graham*!'

Rick's eyes widened and Maddy couldn't help noticing that up close, and when he wasn't scowling, they were very nice eyes—grey with unusual little flecks of vivid blue. 'The woman in the shop?'

She nodded.

'So you know the bride quite well?'

Bride? The word brought sudden, stinging tears to her eyes. Six weeks ago she had been dreaming of being a bride. They hadn't quite set a date. Byron hadn't wanted to commit himself to a definite time frame. There were so many things to consider, he'd said. But still she'd been dreaming of an elegant white gown and a happy country-style wedding at home on her parents' farm.

'Yes.' Maddy hugged her folded arms across her chest

and drew in an angry breath, which emerged seconds later as a long, frustrated sigh. 'Since the eighth grade when I arrived at boarding school. I really don't know why I hadn't already expected this. Cynthia has always wanted everything I ever wanted.' She outlined for Rick a potted history of Cynthia's competitive endeavours over the past decade.

Rick slanted her a sardonic half-smile. 'She sounds like a real honey.'

His sarcasm was like balm to her smarting wounds. 'Oh, she's a sweetie,' Maddy agreed. 'The only area where she couldn't compete with me was music.' Maddy couldn't resist a tiny grin. 'I'm no singing star, but Cynthia didn't have a musical bone in her body. At university she auditioned for our college choir—after I was accepted, of course. But the conductor told her she should confine her vocal talents to the bathroom, but to ensure that it had been soundproofed first.'

Rick grinned back at her. 'That's better,' he said. 'Just keep thinking nice warm and fuzzy thoughts about the two of them and then you'll be able to pull it off.'

Maddy raised startled eyes to his. 'Pull what off?'

'Why, providing the flowers for their wedding, of course.'

Maddy shrank away from him as if he'd been going to strike her. 'What? You've got to be joking! There's no way I would even dream of going near that wedding. I don't even want to organise for anyone *else* to do it!'

Rick grunted his disapproval and slid lower on the sofa, stretching his long legs before him. 'That's a pity.'

Maddy jumped up, angrily tossing her curls. 'A pity?' she cried. 'What would you know about this? Have you any idea what's involved in organising all the flowers for someone's wedding?'

'Tell me.'

She threw her arms wide open to try to convey the enormity of the task. 'First of all I'd have to have them both—possibly a bridesmaid or two or even Cynthia's mother as well—here at my flat for a consultation. Normally people come to the shop, but Byron knows I always bring special friends in here and make a little social occasion of it, so that's what he'd expect. And while I showed them albums of examples and discussed all the different bouquet choices they would be billing and cooing all over each other! Then there'd be endless phone calls and—and decorating the church and the reception venue on the day!' Maddy shuddered. 'No one would expect me to do all that. Not for *them*!'

'Obviously Byron does.'

His casual reply infuriated her. She clenched her fists. How could she expect this stranger to understand or care about her finer feelings?

'But I don't owe Byron anything!'

Rick's puzzled gaze rested on her and Maddy felt the colour rise and fall in her cheeks. 'No, you don't owe him anything,' he reassured her. 'This Byron fellow is obviously a first-class fool. But you look like you've got plenty of spunk. I'm sure you can hold your own in love and war, Maddy.'

'I wouldn't be so certain,' she answered softly.

'Come on. You're not going to let one whimper from your ex-fiancé send you crumpling in a heap like paper thrown on a fire.' Rick raked a hand through his hair. 'I kind of understand how you feel. In my line of work, I've seen plenty of defeated people. I've watched people fight and struggle for basic rights, only to be rejected once too often. That's when they give up.'

'Can you blame them?'

'Not really,' Rick admitted. 'But that's what's so good about my work. Because it's at that point that *sometimes*, by exposing the injustice, my film crew and I have been able to make a difference.'

Maddy had to admire Rick's zeal. She could tell he genuinely cared about his work. But she didn't see how her little problem was quite in the same league.

'You'd be playing right into Byron and Cynthia's hands if you let them know they've hurt you,' he told her. 'From what you've said, I think this Graham woman would enjoy knowing you were suffering.'

Maddy sat down again and met his grey gaze. She swallowed at the impact it had on her at this close distance. 'Cynthia would certainly love it!' she agreed.

She saw his serious expression brighten. 'Then rise above her!' he cried, thumping the sofa with a clenched fist. 'Show her you don't care. Don't let either of them see that you're hurting at all. I promise you, it will feel like a victory.'

Maddy narrowed her eyes as she considered his advice. 'I don't know.' Her voice was low and uncertain.

Rick's clenched hand reached out to trace her cheek with his knuckle. Maddy was surprised by his sudden show of tenderness. It must have startled him too. Abruptly, he rose to his feet. 'Think about it. It's up to you, of course, but my advice would be to take the wind out of their sails. Show them you don't give a damn. Certainly don't lose any sleep over them. They sound like they deserve each other.'

'I will think about it,' she said, standing beside him and following him to her door. 'Thanks, Rick.'

'Thank you for the dinner.'

'Perhaps—another time—I could cook you a proper meal. I rather like cooking.'

'Part of the little home-maker package?' Rick asked.

'I guess so,' she said, then smiled. 'Just look what Byron's missing out on.'

He drew up his shoulders in an exaggerated shrug. 'His loss. Just don't let him gloat, by acting like a victim.'

He let himself out of her flat quickly.

Maddy thought about Rick's advice all night long. 'Don't lose any sleep over them', he'd said. Well, that was impossible. Not just because she was upset about Byron and Cynthia. Rick upset her, too. He was such a disturbing mixture. Tonight he'd shown her little glimpses of a new-age, sensitive male and yet all week he'd behaved like a primitive Neanderthal caveman, offering her no more than a frown and a grunt.

If she took away his good looks, all that was left was a stubborn, impossible male—who occasionally, out of the blue, seemed unexpectedly concerned and considerate. The last point Rick had made certainly rang true. In response to Cynthia and Byron, she *was* behaving like a victim.

Somewhere around three a.m. it finally started to make sense. It was time she took control of her life again. And, yes, she would make a start by doing the flowers for Byron Black's wedding! The Black wedding! She could almost dredge up a giggle. It sounded so macabre. As a few more wicked ideas began to blossom, she almost looked forward to the task. But, she thought as she drifted off to sleep at last, she would need a little help from the man upstairs.

'They're coming next Wednesday at five-thirty p.m.,' Maddy announced to Rick towards the end of the following week. 'Oh, and I've brought you some chicken cacciatore.'

Once again she was standing outside his flat and he was staring back at her, looking grim and a touch confused. 'Run that by me again, please.'

'Sorry,' Maddy apologised, realising she was gabbling. 'Let me start over. Number one, how's Sam?'

He folded his arms across his wide chest. 'Coming along better than expected.'

'Wow, that's great! I should think hardly anyone gets to exceed a doctor's expectations!'

'Yeah, I guess that's so.' Rick's scowl softened and, like the sun peeping over the horizon, his face brightened. Maddy found herself staring at him. How amazingly good it felt inside to see his slow, sexy smile.

She proffered a covered dish wrapped in a gingham tea towel. 'Second thing, I made a chicken casserole for my brother Andy and saved some for you.'

'That's very kind of you.' He accepted the dish, his frown back in place.

Maddy's empty hands dropped onto her hips. 'But the big news is...that Byron and Cynthia have made an appointment to consult about the flowers.'

Rick's eyes gleamed. 'Good. So you're taking them on.'

'I am.' Maddy straightened her shoulders; she was still trying to convince herself that she could pull this off. 'And I feel quite ready for their visit. Or at least I will when I've finished my preparations.'

'I wouldn't go to too much trouble if I were you. From what you've told me, they don't deserve any extra trimmings.'

'No, but I do,' Maddy replied with careful emphasis.

'Pardon?'

'The preparations are for *me*. I need to bolster my morale so I can face them both and keep my chin up,' she explained.

He was curious now. She could tell, because he was forgetting to frown at her.

'So what did you have in mind?'

Maddy smiled. 'I need to do some reconnaissance.'

Rick shook his head as he lounged against the doorjamb. 'You've totally lost me again.'

'I need your help. Actually, I need to inspect your flat.'

'Like hell you do.' His scowl deepened.

'I'm sorry, but it's important. It's necessary research. I need to see how a man lives,' Maddy told him cheerfully.

Rick looked so startled, Maddy thought he was going to drop the casserole dish.

She shifted her weight from one foot to the other. She was getting tired of hovering in the hallway. Rick Lawson certainly didn't go out of his way to be hospitable. 'When Byron and Cynthia come. When they arrive at my place, I have to pretend that I have a—new lover. You know, a live-in lover. Remember? I told Cynthia in the shop that day that he was moving in.'

'So you're going to keep this subterfuge going as a morale booster, are you?' Rick drawled.

Maddy hesitated. If Rick was going to be negative or cynical about her plans, she would get nowhere. 'Well, yes. I couldn't bear to have Cynthia catch me out. And Byron and Cynthia will get the picture that I'm not jealous much more clearly if I have my own gorgeous hunk of live-in masculinity, won't they?'

'I—I guess so.' Rick stared at her and she could have

sworn his jaw thrust forward slightly. 'So, where exactly does my flat fit into all of this?'

'Oh, Rick, please let me in and then I'll explain. After all, you bounced into my flat unannounced the other night and all's fair in love and war.'

He stood frowning for a little longer before he finally shrugged and stepped back, gesturing for her to enter. 'I can't promise you'll be impressed.'

'I'm not expecting to be impressed,' said Maddy, beaming triumphantly as she followed Rick into his lounge room. 'I have two brothers and their rooms have always looked like war zones. But I wasn't sure if they were typical of the male species.'

Halfway across his lounge room, Rick paused. 'So you've never been in another man's apartment?'

Her confidence faltered. 'N-no. Not alone with a man who lives—alone.''

'There must have been boyfriends?'

'At uni I lived in a residential college—so did most of the guys I dated. I occasionally saw their rooms, but it's not quite the same.'

'What about Dracula? What's his name again?'

'Byron.' She shot him a drop-dead look. 'He lives with his mother. And she still does everything for him.'

One of Rick's eyebrows rose and he smiled at her. 'One might almost feel sympathy for Cynthia.'

Maddy allowed herself a small chuckle. 'Yes. She might be in for one or two surprises.'

'Perhaps you had a lucky escape.'

'Perhaps…'

By the time Maddy had journeyed through Rick's flat and reached his kitchen, it was her turn to be surprised. His flat was amazingly neat. Neat wasn't really the word for it. It was spartan. 'Your—your flat is virtually empty!' she cried in dismay.

'Welcome to masculine perfection,' he said with a laugh.

She rolled her eyes.

'Well,' he went on defensively, 'these are only temporary digs. This isn't my home, you know. Not that I really have a home anymore.' He paused and frowned. 'I'm never settled in one place for long. I couldn't get a furnished apartment close to the hospital for just a few weeks and I didn't want to waste money getting a whole lot of unnecessary furniture.' Setting the casserole dish down on a kitchen bench, he turned to her. 'So, Ms Delancy, what exactly did you want to know about male habitats?'

Maddy chewed her soft lower lip. She'd been afraid Rick would make fun of her scheme and it seemed her fears were warranted. Still, she was committed to this appointment with Byron and Cynthia now, and so she had to press on. 'Well, you said yourself the other night that there was no sign of a man in my flat, so I want to plant evidence of a man's existence about the place. I guess if you can't—or won't—help me I can make it up myself—a football sweater draped over a chair, joggers under the sofa, shaving gear in the bathroom.'

'Bathroom?' His forehead wrinkled in surprise. 'Do you need to go into that much detail?'

'Definitely. I'm sure Cynthia is the type to investigate the bathroom cabinet while she visits—just so she can check out every intimate detail. If she had time she would probably snoop around the bedroom too.'

'What might she hope to find there?'

To her annoyance, Maddy felt her cheeks burn. 'I was

actually thinking of pyjamas.' She looked at him shyly. 'You don't happen to have a spare pair, do you?'

'To leave poking out from under your pillow?'

'Something like that.'

'Sorry,' Rick grinned. 'I never use them. Can't help you there at all.'

'Oh...' Maddy made a show of examining her nails while she tried to banish thoughts of Rick between the sheets and without pyjamas.

'I'm starting to get the picture.' He looked around his bare kitchen. 'Would you like some coffee? Or perhaps a beer?'

'Coffee would be lovely.'

He switched on his electric kettle before grabbing a teaspoon to lever the lid off a tin of instant coffee. 'I'm afraid there's nothing fancy here.'

'Instant's fine,' she told him. With something of a start, she realised that anything was fine when Rick was being friendly and cooperative like this. Just watching him fill mugs with steaming water filled her with warm, bubbling happiness.

Rick held a mug in each hand and indicated the lounge room with his shoulder. 'Take a seat in there and I'll see if I can come up with any helpful hints.'

There was still only the one dilapidated director's chair in the room and Rick sat cross-legged on the rather unattractive carpet.

Feeling like a rather hesitant Goldilocks, Maddy tried the chair. 'I'll sit on the carpet, too,' she offered. 'I feel a bit elevated up here.'

It was only after she'd lowered herself to the floor that Maddy remembered she was wearing a very short skirt. She manoeuvred herself into the most demure position possible with her knees tightly together and her legs tucked to one side. With one hand, she tugged at her tartan skirt to hold it in place, while with the other she accepted the coffee. 'So, have you any bright ideas?'

For several long seconds Rick seemed to be having trouble coming up with an answer. 'Er, um golf clubs.'

'Golf clubs? You want me to park some golf clubs in a corner somewhere?'

'They'd impress Byron, wouldn't they?'

'Probably, if they were really good quality, but I don't know where I'd get them from.'

'I'll see what I can do.'

'You play golf?'

Rick shook his head. 'No, I've never had time to pick up the skills. As far as I'm concerned golf is a good walk interrupted. But I have a couple of friends who are mad keen golfers. I'm sure one of them will help out.'

'That would be great. Thanks. Any other suggestions?'

Rick smiled and his grey eyes twinkled. 'Well, there's one obvious give-away.'

'Yes?'

'The toilet seat has to be up.'

Maddy laughed. 'Of course! Goodness, I should have thought of that after living with two brothers for seventeen years.'

'Some masculine magazines scattered—if you can bear to clutter that stunning flat of yours.'

Maddy took a sip of her coffee. It was very strong. 'Yes, magazines are a good idea. What sort do you think would be best?'

Rick leaned back against the ugly yellow wall, raised one knee and rested his elbow on it. 'It could be anything from a mag about game fishing to an almanac of British vintage motorcycles. I guess it rather depends on this lover of yours.' His level gaze held hers. 'So tell me, Maddy, what is your idea of the ultimate lover?'

Maddy felt herself blushing again. When she'd headed for Rick's flat, she'd never intended to end up discussing her ideas about men. 'I—I don't know,' she stammered. 'He's perfect of course. The kind of guy any girl would swoon over.'

Rick's eyes held hers for an uncomfortably long time. 'Go on,' he said at last. 'Describe him.'

'Well—um—he's athletic, likes to keep fit,' she began self-consciously.

Rick nodded, his grey eyes barely concealing amusement. She decided to put him in his place. He was wearing the same faded tracksuit he'd worn when she'd brought him the irises. She ran a deliberate eye over his clothes. 'Of course, he dresses well.'

Rick's eyes still held hers, his expression challenging.

'He earns a decent salary,' she continued. 'He isn't afraid to do some of the cooking. And he's fun to be with—as well as thoughtful and romantic.'

'Not a problem,' Rick drawled with a confident grin. 'Sounds like your average Australian bloke.' He drained his coffee and then his eyes narrowed. 'Just so I'm clear on this, can you define the female's view—correction, *your* view—of "romantic"?'

Maddy clutched her mug to her chest. Surely this discussion was becoming more in-depth than was necessary? Once upon a time, she would have had no trouble answering that question, but now she was less sure. When Byron had produced surprise tickets to the ballet, she'd thought it was a romantic gesture until she'd discovered they were cast-offs from his mother. Most girls found gifts of flowers romantic, but her business thrived on that. It wouldn't work for her.

At that very moment she was feeling absurdly romantic, sitting on Rick's mouldy carpet and sipping his bitter coffee. 'I—I guess it depends on the man,' she said hurriedly, her mind searching desperately for a feasible answer. 'He does whatever suits his temperament. It could be anything—maybe writing poetry or love songs or—or a dinner by candlelight on a secluded balcony.' She put the mug down beside her on the carpet and folded her hands in her lap. She kept her eyes lowered. 'I guess it's only limited by his imagination.' Then she forced a light laugh and looked at Rick again. 'Or in this case, unfortunately, by my imagination.'

Then she wished she could take back her words. Just talking to Rick Lawson about her imagination seemed to unleash ridiculous, teasing fantasies. And there was no way she could afford to blush again.

Rick considered her words for several moments. 'Imagination can be dangerous, Maddy.'

She was stunned. Was he reading her mind? The unwanted blushes arrived with relentless punctuality.

His eyes were fixed on hers so intently, she wondered if he was angry with her. 'So let me get this straight,' he drawled after some time. 'Love poetry and candlelit dinners on—what was it—secluded balconies?'

Maddy gulped. 'It doesn't have to be poetry...'

Rick's smile teased her. 'What else did you have on your list? Songs? Not too many blokes sound romantic when they try to sing.' He scratched his head and frowned as if this whole issue was intensely serious and very puzzling. 'I understand why the balconies need to be secluded,' he said with a suggestive wink. 'And I know poetic guys have always had a lot going for them. But I'm surprised you haven't mentioned muscles, brawn...bedroom eyes... They're not a turn-on for you, Maddy?'

'I—I don't remember saying that,' she stammered. 'But gorgeous guys are not always...romantic. Romantic men are...are thoughtful.' She felt distinctly hot and bothered having this conversation with this particular man. Superbly built, but decidedly offhand and brusque, he broke all the silly definitions of romance she'd just outlined and yet still managed to make her heart flutter quite ridiculously.

'So this Byron fellow of yours—he did all these romantic things for you? Wrote you poetry and wined and dined you in secluded little corners?'

Maddy quickly sipped her coffee. It had cooled and tasted terrible, but at least it helped her to cover her confusion. When she thought about her time as Byron's fiancée, she couldn't remember any little romantic gestures. He'd taken her to restaurants certainly, but usually as part of 'the gang'. He'd spent nights at her apartment...

Rick was waiting for an answer. 'I don't think Byron's romantic technique is any of your business,' she told him huffily. 'We need to stick to practicalities.' Her voice was slow and unsteady. 'So, would you mind if I borrowed your shaving gear for an hour or so next Wednesday? It would be good to have some male deodorant, too.'

Rick ran his hand slowly over his chin and his eyes held a teasing glint as he considered the matter. 'I guess I could release such essential equipment for a very short time.'

Maddy smiled. 'Thanks, Rick. You don't happen to have a football jersey, do you?'

'Sorry, no. But I do have a very ancient rowing one, if that's any use to you.'

'Rowing? Yes, please. That's sure to impress Cynthia.'

'Would you like a photo? Thanks to Sam, I have a few on hand. I could autograph it: "To my darling Maddy".'

'Oh, er, I don't know.' *His darling Maddy?* Why did those simple words send her heart into overdrive? She knew he was joking, playing along with her game of pretence, but hearing Rick say those words made her heart beat so violently, she was afraid he would hear its drumming. How could she let one little throwaway line send her into such turmoil?

'It would clinch the authenticity angle,' he added.

'I—I guess so.'

Rick's fingers raked through his hair. 'It's no skin off my nose. I don't care what you do with it afterwards. You could burn it as soon as you're finished with it.'

Maddy plucked a loose strand of carpet. She must remember that accepting his photo was all part of the game. *It meant nothing!*

She hadn't realised how long she was taking to answer him and was shocked when he jumped to his feet suddenly. 'No, my pic wouldn't be a good idea,' he growled.

'Oh?' Maddy tried to hide her disappointment. Once she'd got over the initial shock, she had really warmed to the notion.

'You wouldn't want this to get too complicated and if Byron recognised me, well, things could get kind of awkward.'

Somehow Maddy doubted that Byron watched documentaries about famine in Third World countries or military coups in far-flung trouble spots. When she thought about it, he was a pretty shallow, narrow-minded sort of fellow. She was beginning to wonder exactly why she'd once found him so thrilling. On the other hand, she reflected with a pang of regret, she could appreciate that Rick Lawson would not want his public image entangled in her private affairs any more than was absolutely necessary. And, she reminded herself with a stab of dismay, he had his own girlfriend lying in hospital, so he certainly wouldn't want to become mixed up with somebody else.

'We'll drop the photo idea, then,' she said. 'I'll rack my brains to come up with a couple more details, but I think we've got the basics established for a pretty convincing deception.' Impulsively, she stood on tiptoes. Then froze. She'd been about to drop a reassuring kiss on Rick's cheek, just as she might have kissed her brothers, but at the last minute it didn't seem such a good idea.

Something warned her that kissing Rick Lawson—even a light kiss on the cheek—would be nothing like kissing a brother. She stepped away quickly. 'Thanks a lot for your promise to help, Rick.'

His gaze touched hers, then withdrew. 'My pleasure,' he grunted.

So that was how it was going to be, Maddy thought as she headed back down the stairs. Rick was back to scowling and grunting again. But she mustn't let it bother her. Surely any amount of scowling would be worthwhile if Byron and Cynthia were taken in by her little subterfuge?

CHAPTER THREE

'SO WE'LL settle for the orchids?' Maddy looked up from her display book to check Cynthia and Byron's reactions. They nodded simultaneously. 'I'm sure you'll be happy with your choice,' she told them. 'An orchid wedding is always very elegant.'

She rested her elbows on the table, let out a deep breath and felt her facial muscles relaxing into a smile. Things were looking good. It appeared more and more likely that the plan would work. Cynthia and Byron had been in her flat for over an hour. The flowers for the wedding were more or less settled and Cynthia's initial gloating smirk had been wilting for some time. Barely concealing her secret delight, Maddy watched as her visitors' eyes kept wandering to the subtle little clues she'd planted around the room.

Some of the props were not so very subtle, she had to admit. Byron had almost tripped over Rick's hiking boots and Cynthia had had to delicately remove his rowing jersey from her chair before she sat down. But her blue eyes had widened and her carefully painted lips had pursed as she'd surreptitiously read the details of Rick's rowing history embroidered on the pocket.

Also courtesy of Rick, some books about politics in Asia and the Middle East rested on the coffee table beside a stack of upmarket magazines Maddy had found in a second-hand shop. She'd taken pains to arrange the reading material with just the right air of casual elegance.

Byron had frowned when he'd first seen them. And his gaze had returned more than once to the impressive set of golf clubs, which hung next to Maddy's raffia sunhat on a brass hook just inside the front door.

Quite early on in the session, Cynthia had made the expected trip to the bathroom and Maddy had noticed with a surge of wicked pleasure, that she returned looking rather pale and tight-lipped. Somehow, her ash-blonde beauty seemed tarnished by her discoveries of a man in Maddy's life.

'I'm glad we've got these flowers sorted out, then,' Maddy said as she made a final note in her order book. 'Your bouquets should look super on the big day. It won't be easy to get everything ready in such a hurry, but I'm fairly confident.'

'I hope having our wedding so soon won't be too difficult for you,' said Cynthia. 'But you know Byron.' Her lips stretched into a wide smile. 'Once he sets his mind on wanting something, he can be very impatient.'

'Of course,' replied Maddy coolly, feeling her hackles rise.

Once he set his mind on Cynthia, he was very impatient! She ground her teeth. It wasn't at all how she remembered Byron. A suffocating band of tension tightened around her rib cage. When she'd been engaged to him, he had been forever finding reasons to postpone their wedding date. It had hurt her then, and the recollection was still painful.

And now she had to look on while he favoured Cynthia with a soppy smile that reminded her of a puppy in a pet store longing to be stroked. And in response Cynthia reached across the table and ran a long finger, tipped by a bright red nail, down her fiancé's cheek.

Feeling as cheerful as a hostess at a wake, Maddy

forced herself to address her visitors brightly. 'What can I offer you to eat or drink? Wine, coffee? Chocolate mud cake?'

'Chocolate mud cake!' Cynthia wailed, and her hand flew to her mouth. 'Oh—oh, hell,' she moaned. For several seconds, she swayed in her seat like a drunken sailor while her face turned a dirty, greenish shade. 'Excuse me,' she muttered, grabbing her handbag as she staggered to her feet and headed swiftly down the hall towards the bathroom.

'Goodness!' Maddy shot Byron a questioning look. 'Is Cynthia unwell? You should have said so. I could have changed the appointment.'

Byron squirmed uncomfortably and studied his fingernails. 'She's just been a little off-colour,' he mumbled.

'I'd better see if she needs anything,' Maddy said, standing up.

As she waited outside the closed bathroom door, she heard unmistakable, unpleasant noises coming from inside. Maddy hovered in the hallway until the sounds eventually stopped and she heard taps running.

'Cynthia?' she called as she knocked tentatively. 'Is there anything I can do to help?'

The door opened. Cynthia stood in front of the sink, looking pale and shaken. 'I'll be all right now,' she muttered. She leaned against a towel rail. 'Oh, God! This is awful! I thought it was only supposed to happen in the mornings.'

'M-mornings?' stammered Maddy.

'Yes. It would have to be my luck to get evening sickness as well as morning sickness.' Cynthia closed her eyes and dabbed at her face with a tissue. When her eyes opened, they caught Maddy's expression of open-mouthed horror. 'Lord!' she exclaimed. 'Didn't you know?'

'I—I don't think so. You mean you're pre-pregnant?'

'I sure as hell am,' sighed Cynthia. 'Didn't Byron tell you when he broke off the engagement?'

For the space of several seconds Maddy stared at Cynthia. She felt as if she'd been hurled out of a rocket ship, tumbling without a lifebelt into black, endless space. She was convinced she would never feel solid earth beneath her feet again. 'No, I had no idea,' she whispered at last. 'At—at the time, Byron didn't mention you—or a pregnancy.'

Cynthia shook her head. 'Don't worry. He broke off the engagement just as soon as he discovered I was pregnant.'

'How thoughtful of him,' sniffed Maddy. She was beginning to feel less numb. Shock was giving way to anger. How dared Byron? What a lowlife! How long had he been two-timing her? The rat! The snake! Her teeth clenched hard as she bit off a loud retort.

Cynthia pulled a brush out of her handbag and began to drag it through her long blonde hair as she examined her image in the bathroom mirror. 'I *thought* you might not know.' Her mouth curved into a simpering smile. 'But I must say I don't feel quite so bad about all this now I know you have someone else.'

'Someone else?'

Cynthia's eyes widened as she took out a tube of lipstick. 'Well, darling, the new man living with you of course,' she responded. 'You pointed him out in the shop the other day, remember? I can see he's made himself at home.' She pointed a bright fingernail at the blue and white striped plastic travel pack sitting squarely on top of Maddy's pastel vanity unit. While Cynthia filled in her lips with crimson, Maddy focused on the pack. It was overflowing with razors, a shaving brush and tubes of lathering cream. A large bottle of aftershave stood beside it.

Contrasting with the feminine décor of Maddy's bathroom—pale pink and champagne fittings plus a delicate collection of moisturisers and perfumes arranged on a slim glass shelf—Rick's functional gear screamed *male*!

It looked exactly how Maddy had planned it. 'Oh!' she gasped.

How could she so easily have forgotten her pretend lover? The shock of Cynthia's news had completely stripped her mind of any other thoughts.

After imagining this charade about her lover all week and picturing the scenario in every tiny detail, it seemed impossible that he'd slipped her mind so quickly. Five minutes ago, she'd almost been rubbing her hands with glee to see her plans go so successfully.

But Maddy could never have predicted Cynthia's news. At the mention of her pregnancy, Maddy's enthusiasm for Project Lover had been doused as effectively as a firecracker dunked in water.

Now, with Cynthia's shrewd gaze fixed on her, she struggled to set aside her hurt over Byron's betrayal and to concentrate on 'the plan'. It was more important than ever to completely convince these two that she wasn't hurting at all.

'Of course,' she replied with forced brightness. 'You don't need to feel sorry for me. I found a—a new man quite quickly.'

Cynthia replaced the hairbrush and lipstick and snapped her handbag shut. 'That's great.' She smiled with about as much sincerity as a grinning crocodile. 'I'm so happy for you. You must tell us all about him.'

They walked back into the lounge room to find Byron thumbing through a magazine about vineyards in France. He looked up and shot them both a guilt-ridden grimace. 'Everything OK?' he asked.

'Cynthia's feeling much better,' Maddy told him frostily. But under the icy tone she could feel her temper blazing. She wanted so badly to yell at him. She needed to hurl every accusation and every foul name that had ever been thrown at a two-timing slime bag!

But as she stood there, facing Byron, her chest heaving and her hands clenched, Maddy heard Rick's advice filtering through her anger. 'Don't let him gloat, by acting like a victim.' She took a long, slow breath and she felt a reassuring surge of gratitude for Rick's support. His was the best advice she'd received since the engagement had been broken off and now, as she thought of the way he'd urged her to 'rise above' them, she could feel her courage gathering. She faced Byron with her shoulders back and her head high.

She flashed what she hoped was a hearty smile. 'Now let's see. The offer for light refreshments still holds.'

'Do you have soda and crackers?' asked Cynthia, who still looked quite wan as she sat once more at Maddy's dining table.

'Yes,' Maddy reassured her.

'I'll take you up on that offer of wine,' said Byron.

As she loaded a tray with drinks and glasses, crackers and cheese, Maddy almost gave in to tears. She tried deep breathing to help herself to calm down, but she felt so betrayed *and* so inconsequential. Byron had been able to cast her aside as easily as a fisherman might throw back an undersized fish. And clearly he considered Cynthia a prize catch.

'This new fellow who's moved in,' Cynthia asked as

she returned. 'The new love interest. I didn't get a really good look at him the other day, but we don't know him, do we?'

'I don't think so,' Maddy answered cautiously as she placed a glass of soda on a coaster before her. 'He's only recently returned to Australia from abroad.'

'Is he something of a wine connoisseur?' asked Byron, glancing back at the *Fine Wines* magazines he'd left on the coffee table.

Maddy was about to pour Byron a glass of Chablis. She hesitated before she replied, knowing that she had just decanted the wine from a cheap cardboard cask.

Crossing her fingers and hoping that Byron would never recognise just how ordinary her wine was, she smiled back at him. 'Yes, he's something of an expert.'

Byron sniffed at the glass. Had his nostrils always been that large? Maddy wondered. He took a slow sip of her bargain-basement wine while she held her breath. 'Ah,' he smiled as he lifted the glass to the light. 'That's what I call a classic drop.'

'Glad you like it,' Maddy mumbled, biting down hard on her twitching lips. 'Have some cheese.'

'Tell us some more about the mystery man,' demanded Cynthia. 'My dear, you're practically bubbling with joy. He must be making you very happy.'

'Oh, he is. Believe me, he is.' Maddy forced a bright smile and swallowed a hefty swig of wine.

'Go on,' Cynthia urged, leaning forward on her chair and fixing Maddy with an intense gaze. Maddy knew that look only too well. Cynthia was almost cross-eyed with jealousy.

Touching wood under the table for luck, Maddy ran through the mental list of the outstanding qualities she'd bestowed on her exciting lover. She decided to go for the kill. 'He has a great body,' she said with exaggerated enthusiasm.

'I did happen to notice that,' Cynthia commented dryly.

Byron stared at her, his expression stony.

'He writes truly beautiful poetry for me.'

'How sweet.' Cynthia favoured her fiancé with a narrow-eyed sneer.

'And he just loves to shower me with all sorts of thoughtful little gifts.'

'Really?' queried Cynthia. 'Tell us more.'

'Jewellery, perfume, lingerie…'

'Lucky you.' Cynthia's response was just short of a snarl.

'How does he earn a quid?' asked Byron.

'He's in—in television,' Maddy supplied hastily.

'Oh!' replied Cynthia and Byron in chorus.

Byron's pale blue eyes were bulging more with each new snippet of information. 'Would we have seen him?' he asked.

'Ah—maybe.' Maddy was wondering how far she could safely take this when there was a knock on her door. 'Excuse me,' she murmured, standing up quickly and praying that this visitor would not spoil her plans.

She hurried across the room and edged the door open. *Oh, no!* God was not answering her prayers this evening.

Rick filled her doorway. He beamed at her. 'How did it go?'

She nearly slammed the door in his face. But her flat's front entry was easily visible from her dining table. Maddy stared at Rick and gulped—twice, trying to will him to dematerialise. Miracles were not her strong point and she could feel two sets of eyes boring into her back. Maddy took a deep breath.

'Darling!' she cried, and flung her arms around his neck. Feeling Rick stiffen within her embrace, she hissed in his ear, 'They're still here!'

'Oh!' she heard him exclaim. Then 'O-oh!' again more softly as his arms came around her and his lips lowered to hers.

Maddy was prepared for a friendly smack on the lips. Under the circumstances, she was quite certain that was about the only kind of kiss she could handle.

But Rick was obviously a better actor than she'd realised.

His mouth was warm, firm and confident as it met hers. It claimed and caressed her with mesmerising thoroughness and, to her surprise, she felt herself rising on tiptoes to hold herself more closely against him. When he withdrew slightly, Rick smiled down at her, holding the sides of her face with both hands and looking at her with such genuine tenderness that her heart flipped wildly.

This is enough. You've done well, she told herself, and she tried to pull back. But Rick bent his head towards her once more and before she knew it her lips were parting eagerly and his tongue was tangling with hers in a shockingly intimate, slow dance.

Maddy's eyes shot wide open before they closed blissfully and her arms tightened even further around his neck. He tasted and felt so-o good. Delicious shivers rippled through her as Rick's hands travelled down her back, to secure her hips tightly against his. And her blood pulsed wildly as the hard heat of his body pressed into her.

It was only with the greatest of difficulty that she finally broke away.

Byron and Cynthia were staring at them, their jaws

somewhere near the tabletop. Maddy wondered if she looked as stunned as they did.

'Well, guys,' she said shakily, 'meet Rick.' She reached behind him and pushed the door closed. Then, taking his hand, she led him across the room.

He will never forgive me for this, she thought.

While the introductions were made, Maddy could feel her cheeks flaming. In fact, afterwards she could never quite remember how her legs had carried her. They felt gelatinous. She didn't dare link eyes with Rick. But she could see Cynthia's eyes working overtime, checking him out as if she had X-ray vision, and Maddy was grateful that he'd replaced his beloved old tracksuit with blue jeans and a white T-shirt that showed off his broad shoulders, well-moulded chest and taut stomach. He really matched the splendid description of her lover, and then some.

He took a seat and she hurried into the kitchen to get another wineglass. When she returned and slipped into a seat beside Cynthia, the other woman leaned over and asked in a low hiss, 'Some welcome home. So how are your tonsils?'

Maddy shot her a close-lipped, prim smile. Trust Cynthia to spoil such a beautiful moment with a crude comment. She turned to Rick. 'Wine, darling?'

'Thanks,' he nodded.

'It's a beautiful wine,' enthused Byron, holding out his glass for a refill. 'Very dry and delightfully subtle. I believe you're quite a wine buff, Rick?'

Rick shook his head and Maddy sent him a swift kick under the table.

'Oh, yeah,' he quickly amended. 'I like to think I know a thing or two about fine wines.'

'Can you pick which year this wine is just by tasting it?'

'Let me see,' Rick murmured, raising his glass to his lips and shooting a curious glance Maddy's way. He took a sip of the wine and Maddy held her breath. She saw his mouth twitch. He was about to pull a face, but just in time he managed to turn the grimace into a sickly grin.

'South Australian, isn't it?' Byron asked tentatively, clearly anxious to show some knowledge.

'No, I don't think so, mate. I'd say this little number's from New South Wales—the Hunter Valley,' Rick told him. 'And at a guess I'd say…off hand…' he took another sip and looked at the ceiling thoughtfully. 'My guess is it's a '93.' He sent Maddy a meaningful glance. His message was loud and clear. *The ball's in your court.*

''93? That's exactly right,' chimed in Maddy. She couldn't resist tossing Byron a triumphant grin. 'Rick certainly knows his wines.'

He will definitely never forgive me, she decided.

Cynthia leaned forward to allow Rick a clear view of her cleavage. 'So, Maddy tells us you're in television.'

'Er, yes.' Rick fixed Maddy with a cagey stare and shifted in his seat. 'So how much have you let on, pumpkin?'

Maddy shook her head and held out her hands in a gesture of innocence. Of course she hadn't said anything. So far she'd been very careful to protect his anonymity. After all, one of Australia's best foreign correspondents would hardly want news of romantic entanglement to leak out to the general public.

Especially when the whole affair was one big charade.

'Rest easy, Rick,' Cynthia purred. 'Maddy's been very discreet.'

'Discreet, eh? That's my girl.' He helped himself to a cracker and cheese.

'Rick, where have I seen you? Should we recognise you?' asked Byron. 'Are you an on-screen man?'

Maddy chewed her lip, wondering desperately how she could help Rick out of this corner.

'No particular reason why you should know me, old pal,' Rick responded. 'Unless you take an interest in world affairs.'

Byron frowned and eyed Rick warily, as if he couldn't quite tell if he'd been insulted. He dropped his gaze as he fiddled with the stem of his wineglass, then grinned as a bright idea struck. 'I've got it! You're the guy in those airline ads!' He looked around at everyone, clearly delighted with his discovery.

Maddy's eyes never left Rick's. And his had darkened to a stormy charcoal-grey as he favoured the other man with a long-suffering smile. 'Now, that's enough about me.' His tone was clearly dismissive. His next words were even more so. 'Sweetheart,' he drawled, 'you should have told me you'd invited our guests to stay on for dinner.'

'Dinner?' Maddy echoed, her mouth remaining open as she digested Rick's blatant rudeness. He couldn't have made his wishes more obvious if he had leapt to his feet and yelled at Byron and Cynthia to get lost. And that, she thought with a rueful sigh, was probably the only way they would get rid of this insensitive pair.

But to her surprise Byron took the hint. He probably wasn't enjoying himself much anymore now he'd actually met Rick and suspected that Maddy was quite contented. He jumped to his feet. 'Sorry, mate,' he said.

'Much as we'd love to, Cynthia and I can't stay to dinner. We've been here much longer than we expected. And, well, we've places to go...' He grabbed Cynthia's hand and dragged her out of her seat.

'It's been wonderful to meet you, Rick,' she said, flashing him a wide, toothy smile.

'Delighted,' murmured Rick. He moved beside Maddy and draped a casual arm across her shoulders. 'I've been looking forward to meeting more of Maddy's friends.'

'Oh, I've just had the best idea!' cried Cynthia, digging a sharp finger into Byron's shoulder. 'We must invite Maddy and Rick to the little get-together your mother's putting on for us. Then Rick can meet the gang!'

'Sure,' agreed Byron with a slight shrug.

'Oh, no! We couldn't,' Rick and Maddy responded in chorus.

'Please, don't say no,' moaned Cynthia. 'It's going to be a lovely party. Two weeks on Saturday. We're having a kind of engagement party and baby shower combined—for all the people we can't invite to the wedding.'

'Baby shower?' Rick echoed. 'What baby?' He turned to stare at Maddy in obvious dismay and she could see a small muscle twitching in his cheek.

Oh, Lord! Maddy felt her lower lip tremble and for a horrible moment she thought she was going to make a fool of herself. 'Cynthia and Byron have some rather special news.'

'How long—I mean—when did this happen?' Rick took a menacing step forward, his hands balling into fists and his eyes darting accusingly from Byron to Cynthia and then flashing to Maddy. But nobody moved and nobody spoke.

Oh, heavens, Maddy thought wretchedly. What did Rick expect from this pair? Confession time?

'So you'll come?' asked Cynthia with a forced smile, filling the awkward silence, as if she had absolutely no idea what could be upsetting Rick. 'I'm sure Maddy's dying to show you off to everyone.'

Maddy's heart took a dive. She stared at Rick, trying to gauge his reaction. An angry flush crept along his cheekbones and his lips were compressed into a grim downward curve. Good grief! For an embarrassingly long time, he stood there, looking as if he wanted to smash Byron's teeth in.

Maddy reached up and patted his arm, trying to calm him, although her own stomach was churning. 'Rick is very busy,' she told Cynthia. *Not to mention the fact that he already has a girlfriend.* 'I don't—'

'We'd love to come to your do,' Rick interrupted.

Maddy made a soft sound of protest, but to her surprise he quickly silenced her with a finger on her lips. 'Sweetheart,' he breathed, 'you know how keen I am to meet all your friends.'

Her brown eyes widened even as her brows drew down in a questioning frown.

'Two weeks on Saturday? We'll be there,' he told Cynthia.

'Wonderful.'

She was almost home free, Maddy thought as she opened the door for her guests to leave...apart from dealing with Rick once this was over.

At last they were gone.

Maddy slipped her arm out of Rick's and shut the door quickly behind the retreating figures. Leaning back against the timber panel, she drew in a deep breath. 'Thank heavens for that!' she sighed, exhaling deeply on a note of sheer exhaustion.

Rick was standing opposite her, staring at her with his hands on his hips and his mouth a grim, hard line. But she shouldn't be looking at his mouth. Disturbing memories of his kiss lingered, making her feel light-headed and quivery. It had been so easy for him to take her in his arms and kiss her as if he really enjoyed it. He'd clearly had lots of practice.

Maddy was quite sure she'd never been kissed quite so thoroughly. And the way she'd kissed him back had startled her, too. Perhaps she'd been carried away by the surprise element—the unexpected enthusiasm of his embrace. For that short time, she'd certainly forgotten all about poor Sam, still in hospital.

But surely Rick hadn't forgotten her?

'That was some act, Rick. Thanks. Thanks a lot.'

'I would like to say it was a pleasure, but meeting that pair of smiling razor blades has not been the highlight of my life.'

Maddy remained leaning against the door, her eyes closed. 'I'm sure Byron's changed,' she said wearily. 'I don't remember him being quite so...so...'

'Shabby, unfair, dishonest...sneaky? There are a lot of words for what he's done to you, Maddy, and I'm only using the most complimentary ones.'

She knew it was true, but it still hurt. The tears still came. Blinking fiercely, she dashed across the room to gather up the empty plates and glasses from the table and carry them through to the kitchen.

Rick followed. 'The audacity of those two to flaunt their betrayal so brazenly! How could they do that to you, Maddy?'

And how on earth did he expect her to answer that? She piled dishes on her draining board with quick, nervous movements.

'They certainly deserve each other,' he continued. 'Byron's the original Mr Smooth—a con man if ever I saw one. And I've seen plenty of those in my time. They're all the same—superficially handsome and smooth, but as trustworthy as a fox in a henhouse.'

With teeth gritted, Maddy stared at her messy sink, keeping her back to Rick while his tirade continued.

'He's a creep, Maddy—absolute pond scum. Hell, anyone who could pull a stunt like that is lower than a snake's belly.'

'That's enough! I get the message, OK?' An embarrassing sob broke from her lips.

Rick's expression softened. He stepped towards her, his hands outstretched. 'I'm sorry. I'm as bad as he is— hurting you.'

Stumbling past him across the room, Maddy grabbed a tissue from the small box on the opposite bench. 'I'm not really all that upset,' she lied. She blew her nose and tugged another tissue from the box to wipe her eyes. Then she forced her lips into a brave smile. 'I'm going to be all right. It's just that today's been…quite a strain.' She forced her eyes to capture his gaze and hold it. 'You don't have to come to that party, Rick. I'll understand completely if you'd rather not.'

Rick crossed his arms across his broad chest and looked back down at Maddy through lowered lids. 'I said we'll go. We'll go. Damn it, I've helped whole communities in the past by exposing corruption and betrayal! If attending one little party will help you to find your feet and get on with your life, it's not a lot to ask of a fellow.'

She twisted the tissue with nervous hands. 'Modern women are supposed to be independent and to feel perfectly complete and happy on their own—without a man,' she said. 'I shouldn't really feel the need to pretend I have a—a live-in lover. It's just that Cynthia sets up this dreadful sense of competition. She always has.'

'Of course she has!' exclaimed Rick angrily, his grey eyes smouldering. 'And, we're going to beat her once and for all at her own game! This party should clinch it.'

'You don't mind if everybody thinks you're my...my lover?' She struggled to keep the note of pleasure from creeping into her voice.

She felt the pressure of his gaze studying her intently.

'I don't think it will be a problem. It's not as if we're announcing any long-term commitment. People might just assume we're enjoying a brief affair.'

'But what about Sam?'

He looked at her, his expression startled. Then his face relaxed into a slow, reassuring smile. 'Don't you worry about Sam. That's my problem.' He switched his glance away from her, and seemed incredibly interested in the picture on her wall calendar of an English country garden. When he looked at her again, he shrugged and sent her an encouraging smile. 'I'll be off again on another assignment soon. And once we've convinced this pair that you're not pining away or devastated, then we'll all be able to put this whole episode behind us and get on with our separate lives.'

CHAPTER FOUR

'Do you agree that's the way it will be?' Rick asked Maddy. 'I'll come to this party with you, we'll put on a damn good show and then...' he waved his hand in the air '...we say goodbye?'

'Yes.' The single syllable left her lips in a husky whisper tinged with tears. She reached for another tissue and blew her nose loudly, then curved her mouth into a tight little smile.

Rick looked at her sharply then stepped towards her. He reached out as if to comfort her, but he must have changed his mind. His hand fell to his side. 'You're a plucky little thing, Maddy.'

'Plucky?' she exclaimed. 'Plucked would be a better description. I feel so exposed—like a naked, plucked chicken.'

'That's why I say you're brave. It takes guts to face up to the kind of disaster Cynthia and Byron have landed on you.'

His words made her feel so much better than they should. Maddy had a dreadful suspicion she was confusing Rick's offhand offer of help with a gesture of genuine concern. She must remember it was only an act. 'I owe you so much for that performance tonight,' she said.

He swallowed. 'You're quite a convincing actor yourself, Ms Delancy. The way you kissed me back was—' he seemed to hesitate over his words '—convincing.

You're a convincing kisser. There are no other words for it. An Oscar-winning performance.'

To her alarm, Maddy felt a crimson stain creep up her neck and into her cheeks. She turned away from him and ducked her head, while she forced herself to forget about that kiss. 'How can I begin to repay you? Can I offer you dinner? I have some nice marinated beef strips.'

Rick chuckled. 'Beef strips? You really are a practical soul, Maddy.' He paused and looked at his watch. 'Now, I'm sure the beef would be delicious, but I really need to pay Sam a quick visit. I've been caught up with business today and I haven't been to the hospital yet.'

'I can fix a Thai-style stir-fry and have it ready for when you get back, then.'

Frowning, Rick's eyes held hers as he considered her offer. 'I can just picture you staying back in your little kitchen, rustling up a tasty meal. But you'd be alone and mooning over...you know who. I've got a better idea. Why don't you come with me?'

'To visit Sam?'

'Yeah. A change of scenery and a change in conversation is good for a recuperating patient.'

Maddy hesitated. She wasn't sure that she wanted to meet Rick's partner. It would make this whole pretend-lover scheme so much more difficult if she came face to face with his proper girlfriend. Even though Maddy knew her relationship with Rick was only pretence, she would feel somehow that she was cheating on the woman.

She could see Rick was looking at her expectantly, waiting for her answer. 'I'm not sure if it's such a good idea, Rick. I mean...does Sam know about me? Does she mind that you're helping me out?'

His eyes glittered with a flash of amusement and a corner of his mouth twitched. 'I've mentioned you,' he replied. 'And I've told you before, I'll be the one to worry about Sam. Let that be my problem. You have enough of your own.' He paused and rubbed his chin thoughtfully. 'How about we do a deal? I'll help you out with this party if you'll come and talk about your business—the weddings and functions side of it—with Sam.'

'Well, yes. I could do that. It's a fair deal,' she said.

'And perhaps you could also have a break from cooking. We could snatch a bite to eat somewhere on the way home.'

She felt her features break into a wide smile. His lightly offered invitation made her unexpectedly happy. Perhaps she was looking way too delighted. Rick was staring at her strangely.

'I'll be ready in two ticks,' she told him. And she was as good as her word, returning after a quick sortie around her flat with a large woven bag hanging from one shoulder. 'I baked some ginger nut biscuits the other night,' she said, patting the bag. 'Do you think Sam would like some?'

'Sure to. The hospital tucker's not too impressive.'

She scooped up the pile of magazines from the coffee table. 'What about these? Do you think she'd find any of them interesting?'

'We can take them along. They can always be passed on to other patients.'

'OK.' Maddy flashed another of her delighted smiles.

They left the flat. Outside in the little hallway beside her shop, Maddy paused and fished around in her bag for her keys. 'Hold this bag for a second,' she told Rick. 'I just want to check something in the shop.' Scant minutes later, she emerged, her arms overflowing with bunches of fragrant flowers. 'Those irises you took Sam would have died long ago,' she said as she rejoined him. 'I should have thought to send more flowers before now.'

'Well, you're certainly making up for it,' Rick laughed as she handed him an armful of blooms.

As they walked towards the hospital, the city throbbed with its early evening beat. Rivers of cars poured in every direction. Horns honked, tyres swished, brakes screeched. A siren sounded somewhere in the distance. Everywhere, above and around them, lights flickered or glowed against the gathering purplish-black of night—headlights, streetlights, traffic lights and neon signs.

Maddy walked along the footpath beside Rick and was shocked by the happiness that bubbled through her veins. She was half afraid her feeling would burst out in the form of little skips, but somehow she managed to walk at a normal, sedate pace. Her bulging Kenyan bag swung from Rick's shoulder and they both carried bright bunches of roses, carnations, gardenias and baby's-breath.

They arrived in Sam's ward.

Maddy looked around uncertainly and frowned. 'Rick, this is a men's ward.'

He glanced sideways at her startled face and slanted her a sly grin. But before she could question him further he placed a hand at the small of her back and ushered her through a doorway.

'Struth, Rick!' a man sitting up in the bed exclaimed. 'What have you brought me? Paradise?' His grin was so wide, Maddy thought his face would split in two.

In stunned silence, Maddy followed Rick across the room to stand by the bed.

Rick's eyes lingered on her face for a moment before

he grinned back at his friend. 'Sam, meet Madeline Delancy. Maddy, my partner in crime, Sam Chan.'

'So this is the famous flower lady.' The patient's accent was pure Australian, his features classic Chinese. He grinned broadly. 'Stone the crows, you sure are a sight for sore eyes, Maddy.'

Maddy felt her smile waver. She rounded on Rick, shaking her head in confusion. 'Sam's a *him*? I mean a man?'

'Yeah,' he said softly. He tilted an apologetic smile towards the patient.

'I thought *Sam* was short for Samantha. Why on earth did you let me think he was a she?'

His amused gaze linked with hers and she felt an unexpected ripple of warmth feather down her spine. ''Cause I didn't really think it mattered much one way or the other. It doesn't, does it?'

Maddy blushed. If she'd felt as offhand and casual about Rick as he did about her, it certainly wouldn't matter. A curly question wormed its way into her thoughts. How *did* she feel about Rick? But now was not the time for introspection.

'It certainly matters to me whether I'm a he or a she,' interjected Sam, and they all laughed. 'What have you been doing, Rick? Leading this little lady along?'

It was Rick's turn to look sheepish. 'Not really.' He turned to Maddy and shrugged a nonchalant shoulder. 'You were the one to jump to conclusions, Maddy. You must have an overactive imagination. But until now there didn't seem to be any real need to set you straight.'

Maddy smiled. For some ridiculous reason she was suddenly incredibly glad that Sam was male. She beamed at him. 'Lovely to meet you, Sam. I'll shake your hand just as soon as I find somewhere to put all these flowers.'

Rick quickly deposited his flowers on a chair in the corner of the room. 'Let me take them and I'll hunt down a nurse to give us some vases.'

Maddy watched Rick leave and then turned to Sam. His face creased into another wide grin. She held out her hand and he grasped it firmly.

'I sure am thrilled to meet you,' he said. 'I had a sneaking suspicion Rick was exaggerating when he told me about how pretty you were, but I can see he was holding back.'

'Now, Sam,' Maddy laughed, tamping down the little rush of pleasure she'd felt to hear that Rick had been talking about her. 'I bet you've been flirting shamelessly with the nurses, but I warn you not to start on me.'

'Why? Are you already taken? Has Rick already won your fair heart?'

If Sam hadn't looked so serious, Maddy might have laughed out loud. 'No, of course not. Rick hasn't even tried to win me,' she said with a careless shrug.

'The fool.' Sam shook his head and edged himself higher in the bed so he could lean forward and speak softly. 'You know, he's changed since he met you.' He paused and watched her reaction.

Maddy's heart was racketing around at a hectic pace, but she schooled her features into a smile as noncommittal and enigmatic as Mona Lisa's. It would be absurd to imagine that Rick thought of her as anything more than a neighbour he was prepared to talk to when it suited him.

Sam pressed on as if he was eager to share his thoughts with Maddy before Rick returned. 'He seems happier—like he's shed a huge burden—or found Nirvana.'

'Of course he is, Sam. He's so relieved you're not going to be a paraplegic or anything serious like that. He felt terribly guilty about your accident, you know.'

'Silly coot,' sighed Sam. 'He thinks that I didn't want to go on that last assignment just because I put on a bit of a turn. I admit I'm getting a bit long in the tooth for this crazy game, but there's no way I wouldn't have gone with him. I've never been able to resist the chance of good footage.' He sank back into the pillows and for a moment his gentle face looked regretful, but then he turned back to Maddy, his eyes glinting cheekily. 'I wish I'd had my camera with me tonight when you walked in. You looked out of this world, Maddy, with your dark curly hair all tumbling around your head and your arms full of flowers—like the goddess of dawn or dusk or something. Food for my starving soul.'

Feeling a little overwhelmed by his glowing praise, Maddy pulled the magazines and tin of biscuits from her bag. 'Well, here's food for your starving stomach and mind,' she laughed.

At that moment Rick returned with vases for the flowers. 'Let's hope no one else on this ward gets flowers tonight. I think Sam has the entire supply of vases cornered.' He and Maddy quickly arranged the flowers and, under Sam's direction, placed them at carefully selected vantage points around the stark hospital room.

'I feel like a Hollywood star,' Sam said, looking around at the glowing circle of colour.

Rick drew chairs forward for Maddy and himself and they sat beside Sam's bed.

'So how's the hip, Sam?' Maddy asked.

'I reckon it's just about right as rain,' he beamed. 'I've

started to take a few steps. And my sister's coming up from Woollongong soon to take me home to her place for a spell.' He cocked his head towards Rick as he addressed Maddy. 'This bloke's earned his Florence Nightingale award. Time he had a bit of leave to himself.'

'Sam, you know I...' began Rick but a sudden beeping from his chest interrupted him. He frowned and muttered, 'Excuse me,' then rose from his chair and crossed the room to the doorway.

Maddy smiled at Sam, who wiggled his eyebrows and rolled his eyes as Rick extracted a mobile phone from inside his jacket and began to speak into it in crisp, staccato tones.

'I hope you find something of interest in these magazines,' Maddy said to Sam, hunting desperately for suitable small talk, while she tried to ignore whatever had called Rick away.

'Sure to,' he smiled. 'Even if the stories are boring, old cameramen like me get a thrill out of looking at the pictures.'

They both laughed.

Maddy was about to ask a question about Sam's love of photography when the telephone conversation in the doorway finished as abruptly as it had begun and Rick returned to the bedside. He addressed Sam, his profile stern. 'The boss has arrived from New York. He's got the Lear jet waiting at Eagle Farm airport and he wants me in Sydney this evening.' His eyes flashed to Maddy. 'I'm afraid I'm going to have to get a raincheck on that dinner. When the boss snaps his fingers...'

'You jump to attention,' Maddy quipped, but her heart was plummeting. She managed to nod and to stretch her lips into a smile.

Rick's gaze rested on her smiling lips before he sent her a grimacing smile in return. 'It's either that or I walk the plank.' He tucked the phone back into his pocket.

'So you've got to head off straight away?' asked Sam.

'Afraid so.' But although his voice sounded apologetic Maddy noticed that Rick's eyes gleamed with a boyish, expectant light.

She couldn't help but recognise his excitement. There was no sign of frustration or anger at being summoned unexpectedly. Rick showed no signs of regret whatsoever. Instead his face looked keyed up, stimulated by this turn of events. Maddy felt her teeth bite into her lower lip. He couldn't have looked more alert and ready for adventure if he were 007 called on a mission.

As if suddenly remembering his manners, Rick turned to Maddy. 'Would you like me to walk you home first?'

'No, of course not. I'll be fine,' she said hastily, terribly aware that she must not show any sign of disappointment. She should be grateful for this timely reminder. Rick's original invitation to dine out had merely been an extension of the whole game of pretence, a game that had begun the minute he'd shown up at her front door.

In spite of that kiss...

Rick's mouth had been hungry, intense and devastatingly intimate. She had recognised desire—his and hers. There was no doubting the urgency of his kiss or the hard thrust of Rick's body against hers. But then, she reminded herself, she no longer trusted her intuition where men were concerned. Byron had taught her a hard lesson.

She strengthened her smile. 'I'll stay and chat to Sam for a little while.'

Did she imagine Rick's relief when she let him go without complaint?

'I'm not sure when I'll be back,' he muttered. 'There've been new developments on the Cambodian scene.' His glance held Maddy's. 'Don't forget to have a chat about business with Sam.'

'I won't,' she assured him.

'Give my regards to the boss when you see him,' called Sam as Rick said his farewells and headed out the door.

Maddy felt her smile quiver as he disappeared. It was so obvious that Rick had rushed out of the room as if he couldn't wait to get away. She struggled to submerge her disappointment. And she stamped down quickly on the silly little dreams that had been dancing in the wings of her imagination—foolish dreams of walking back out of the hospital with Rick, of finding an interesting little restaurant, of an intimate dinner for two—going back home together.

She stared at the dozen Valentine heart roses arranged in a green glass vase on the table at the far side of Sam's bed and wished she could feel as happy as she had such a short time before, when she and Rick had arranged those flowers together.

How on earth could she have entertained, for even one second, any thoughts that she meant any more to Rick Lawson than the girl in the flower shop downstairs? Was she so desperate to get over Byron that she imagined the very next man to come along was even remotely interested in her?

Sam's hand patted hers and his eyes narrowed thoughtfully. 'Don't worry,' he said gently. 'He'll be back. Just at the moment my old mate doesn't know what he wants. He thinks the next story is the most important thing in his life. But, trust me, Maddy, our Rick's just on the edge of making a personal discovery that will knock him for six.'

Maddy smiled at Sam sadly, not daring to think about what he might be implying. 'You're an old dreamer, Sam,' she told him. 'But what about your plans? Are you interested in wedding photography? Rick seemed to think that line of work might suit you.'

Sam shook his head as he sank back into the pillows and expelled his breath on a long sigh. 'The boy's dreamin'. Strike me pink, Maddy, I'd go bananas doing that kind of thing.'

'It would be very different from the exciting life you're used to,' Maddy offered tentatively.

'Nah. If I could get my hands on a patch of decent dirt, I'd like to try my hand at something completely different—like farming. My old grandfather used to have this beaut market garden.'

'That would be wonderful,' agreed Maddy with heartfelt enthusiasm. As a fellow green thumb, she understood his love of growing things. She dug into her voluminous bag and extracted a small rectangular box. 'But in the meantime, what are you like at playing Chinese checkers?'

She was rewarded by a face-splitting grin.

When Cynthia's invitation to the party arrived in the mail two days later, Maddy wondered if she should just toss it in the waste basket and forget about it. She had absolutely no idea if Rick would be back in time. And, even if he were, the excitement of his work might have totally eclipsed his desire to help Maddy out of her pathetic little pickle.

But just in case he did sweep in at the eleventh hour

and agree to continue the charade for another evening, Maddy found time to go shopping.

And it was fun choosing between a sophisticated little black dress and a demure blue one, or between a saucy red number and an alluring mossy-green velvet. In the end, she made her decision intuitively, selecting a simple, straight shift with shoestring straps. Made of rosy pink silk, it sported a cheeky strip of sheer pink chiffon across the tops of her breasts.

Once the purchase was made, she hung it away at the back of her wardrobe and tried to forget about it. She rang Cynthia and explained that she couldn't give a definite reply to the invitation just yet.

Cynthia's scepticism was poorly concealed. 'Of course, darling,' she crooned. 'I understand completely about these men of the world. They always have multiple agendas. But do come to our soirée anyway. If Rick does stand you up, I'm sure we'll find another nice little man to partner you.'

Maddy didn't care if Cynthia realised just how roughly she crashed the receiver down. And she tried not to care that she didn't hear from Rick at all during the next week.

On the following Saturday, just over two weeks after Rick had left so abruptly, she dressed for the party, steeling herself to face the ordeal alone.

And it was then Maddy discovered that she *did* care a great deal.

She was very disappointed. She tried to reason with herself that Rick was far too busy with important international concerns to remember one little party in Australia. But she thought he might have at least got a message through to her.

As the silk dress slithered over her body with a cool

whisper, tears sprang to her eyes. It dawned on her that she had bought this dress hoping that Rick would see her in it. Now it seemed a total waste of effort! She knew she looked good. The soft dusty pink suited her colouring perfectly. The dress clung in all the right places and, while the see-through panel across her low neckline was more daring than anything she'd ever worn before, it was also very flattering. She admired the effect of her toenails, painted a rosy pearl colour and peeping out from her strappy dull gold sandals.

Maddy reached for her favourite perfume. Light yet exotic, with the faintest hint of citrus, it made her think of sultry nights on an island in the middle of the Mediterranean. At the very least, its fragrance usually lifted her spirits, but tonight as she sprayed a little to her wrists and neck she felt thoroughly depressed.

The thought of Cynthia's manufactured sympathy and Byron's smug smirk, when she arrived at the party alone, made her feel like throwing up. You're being ridiculous, she told herself and, tamping down her revulsion, she took two sips of cold water, blotted her lips with a tissue and carefully applied her lipstick.

'And,' she told her reflection as she slipped gold hoops into her ears, 'you look damn good.' She wound her curls into a casual knot, high on her head, and secured it with two pins before scooping up her pink and gold tapestry clutch purse.

Time to face the music.

Her small pink van sporting the Floral Fantasies logo was parked in a communal car park in the street behind her flat. Maddy fitted a key to the lock, wishing all the time that the lead weight in the pit of her stomach would dissolve.

She considered her choice of roles for this evening.

Should she try to pose as a frivolous social butterfly, who flitted carelessly from male to male? Or would she be better as a hard-nosed career girl, who didn't give a damn? She narrowed her eyes and lifted her nose in an attempt to look bored and sophisticated. It would be too hard to keep that up all evening. Perhaps she could try to play the part of a serene, self-contained new-age woman? But it wasn't going to be much fun smiling serenely when she felt like the proverbial wallflower—unwanted and embarrassingly alone.

With a deep sigh, she wrenched open the car door and slid into the driver's seat.

'Where are you going?'

The deep voice reached her at precisely the same moment someone grabbed the door's handle, preventing her from slamming it.

'Rick,' she whispered.

It was all the sound she could manage. Her throat closed over as she saw him standing there, towering above her and looking absolutely divine. He seemed more suntanned than she remembered. His teeth gleamed whitely against his dark skin as he smiled uncertainly.

'Am I in time?' he asked, and she noticed he was a touch breathless as if he'd been running.

'For the party?' Her heart was behaving very strangely.

'What else? That's what I've come racing back for,' he said. 'I'm a man who keeps his word, Maddy.' He flashed a sexy, toe-curling grin. 'And you've no idea the strings I've had to pull to get here tonight.'

'You have perfect timing.' She grinned back. 'When did you get back to Brisbane?'

'About forty minutes ago. It was touch-and-go. I really didn't think I was going to make it. Cambodia's a long way from here. I was lucky Cynthia mentioned the date that night at your flat.'

'Oh, Rick, Cambodia? For heaven's sake.' She felt flustered—dizzily happy, amazed—worried that he'd gone to so much trouble. 'It's so good to see you,' was all she could think to say.

He smiled again and her heart thumped even more loudly.

'Hop in.' She reached over and opened the passenger door. Rick looked incredibly handsome in a white shirt, charcoal-grey silk tie and dark trousers, with his coat slung over one shoulder. And as he slid in beside her she caught a whiff of sexy aftershave.

How good it was to see him again! But having him suddenly close beside her in the small van's interior interfered with Maddy's ability to breathe. And when he stared at her intently and remained silent it took all her self-control to refrain from reaching out and touching him.

'How was your assignment in Cambodia?'

The light left his eyes and his jaw hardened. 'Grim.'

'Oh, I'm sorry...' Maddy fiddled with her gear lever.

'Not to worry,' he said, brightening again. 'That job's over and now I want to concentrate on this one.'

Maddy felt her spirits deflate as swiftly as a pricked party balloon. 'You're treating this party like another job?'

His grey eyes met hers warily. 'But isn't that what it is, Maddy? You surely don't think I've been ticking off the days looking forward to Cynthia's party?'

Maddy forced out a cracked little laugh. 'No, of course not.'

His eyes softened and one corner of his mouth

tweaked upwards. 'I like the way you've done your hair.' He fingered a loose curl lightly.

How weak she was. One little compliment and she wanted to curl herself into Rick's arms. But that would certainly frighten him off, she thought ruefully. 'We have a party to attend,' she managed to say in a strangely businesslike voice. She slid the key into the ignition.

'One moment,' said Rick, raising a hand to halt her. 'I need to get my head together about exactly what we're hoping to achieve on this mission tonight.' He leaned back in the seat and his chest expanded as he took a deep breath.

Maddy held her own breath to prevent herself from sighing.

'We're convincing that pair of human piranhas that I'm the love of your life. Correct?'

'Something like that,' Maddy mumbled.

'Hmm,' mused Rick. 'And I haven't had time to do my research.'

'Research?'

'Yes. I never go into a job cold. I haven't a clue how you like your lovers to behave in public.'

If it was possible, the pounding of her heart accelerated. In close proximity, Rick was a health hazard. 'Surely there's no set behaviour…?' Maddy frowned. 'You're teasing me.'

'I'm deadly earnest,' responded Rick, but a gleam in his eye suggested otherwise. 'I mean, tonight's not the night for all that romantic stuff you like. What was it? Poetry and music and candlelit dinners? But I still need to put on a good show. I don't know if you like your guys to be all over you—you know, like a rash—with plenty of fondling and smooching.' He cocked an eyebrow. 'Or if you prefer a more distant, formal manner.'

Maddy clasped her hands tightly together, and was ever so grateful that Rick had no idea how difficult it was for her to hold back from fondling and smooching with him right now. 'Er—I'm sure formal and distant will be fine,' she muttered. 'We really only need to give an impression…'

Rick drummed his fingers on the dashboard. 'From what I've observed, the charming Cynthia doesn't really latch on to subtlety,' he mused. 'Perhaps she'll need more obvious clues, if she's to be convinced that we are—intimate.'

'You—you think so?' Maddy's voice cracked.

He stared ahead at the brick wall at the end of the car park as if he was pondering the situation, then he turned to her, his expression an impossible mixture of boredom and amusement. 'I suggest we adopt a middle-of-the-road approach. How about I promise to remember to hold your hand from time to time?'

Maddy nodded, too breathless to reply, not sure whether to thump him.

'Perhaps I should drop the occasional kiss on that tempting bare shoulder of yours…'

Maddy forgot about thumping him as a blazing wave of heat engulfed her. The very thought of Rick's lips on her skin! She felt her body tremble as desire arced through her with embarrassing force. 'That s-sounds reasonable,' she managed to whisper.

Rick touched her cheek and she knew that a fierce blush blossomed under his hand. 'Or is that going to remind you too much of Bryce…Brian…what's his name again?'

'Byron,' she told him. 'No. I don't think you will ever remind me of him, Rick,' she said softly, hoping her voice didn't reveal too much lust.

His voice deepened. 'I think,' he said softly, his finger trailing across her cheek to outline her jaw, 'that we should dance and that I should hold you very close and...I should most certainly nuzzle your ear.'

'Rick!' Maddy pulled away abruptly, desperately trying to ignore the sizzling sensations his words caused. 'You're flirting with me.'

'Just practising,' he said defensively, holding his hands up to protest his innocence.

Maddy quickly switched on the ignition. *Just get this car moving and concentrate on the traffic,* she warned herself.

'Are you nervous?' Rick asked as she nosed the van out between two concrete pillars.

'A little,' she admitted. In truth, she was positively shaking—had never felt so vulnerable and confused. 'How about you? Any nerves?' she asked, trying to sound casual and light-hearted as she slowed to a halt to check the traffic, before swinging out onto the busy street.

'Calm as a millpond.'

CHAPTER FIVE

'MADDY, dear, so glad you could make it after all.' Cynthia, in a blaze of red silk, rushed forward and crushed Maddy in a bear hug. 'And Rick, darling,' she purred, greeting him effusively and pushing her prominent chest against his as she stood on tiptoes to plant a very familiar kiss on his mouth. 'You're looking just wonderful.' Her voice hummed with a husky burr and she traced the lapel of his jacket with a brightly painted fingernail.

Cynthia's glance swung back to Maddy and her eyes hovered on the sheer fabric at the neckline of her dress. 'Why, Maddy, you—you saucy creature. What are you doing in such a sexy little number? It's not like you at all.'

Maddy felt her teeth clench, but she forced herself to smile. 'Rick begged me to wear this dress,' she said quickly. 'He says...it always drives him wild.' She turned towards Rick.

He was looking a touch shocked. She dug her elbow into his ribs. 'Er—absolutely,' he replied hastily. Then he seemed to warm to his task. He grinned at Cynthia. 'I especially like the way she needs me to zip her into it.'

Maddy's face flamed. She wished she knew something about mental telepathy. *No need to overdo it, Rick.*

Cynthia cackled. 'Our little Maddy's become a sex-pot?' Her face showed utter disbelief. 'So a leopard *can* change its spots?' The smile she offered Maddy was about as warm as frostbite. 'My dear, I'm so pleased to see you aren't moping wretchedly over my naughty boy Byron.'

'I'm—' Maddy flapped her hands as if to dismiss the sympathy. 'I'm quite chipper.'

'And I hope it's not too difficult helping Maddy to pick up the pieces, Rick. I know a romance on the rebound can be a very delicate exercise, very trying.'

To Maddy's surprise, Rick's hand moved to her shoulder and he pulled her close so he could massage the nape of her neck with tantalising, slow strokes. 'Maddy and I are deliriously happy, Cynthia. I'm sure ours is a match made in heaven.' He dropped a sudden kiss on Maddy's cheek.

She gulped. *A match made in heaven?* That was a little over the top. 'But we aren't saying too much just now,' she hastily intervened. 'We—we don't want to take anything away from this happy occasion for you and Byron.'

'Well, Rick, my dear man,' Cynthia drawled. 'I'm going to drag you away from your little piece of hot stuff, so you can meet all our lovely friends. Maddy, sweetie, do be a dear and fetch drinks for Rick and yourself. They're all on that table over there near the window.'

Fuming, Maddy watched Rick saunter off with Cynthia. How dense was he? Surely, if he was supposed to be madly in love with her, he should have shrugged Cynthia aside and insisted on helping her with the drinks?

With gritted teeth, Maddy made her way to the drinks table, observing that Cynthia and Byron were not the most thoughtful hosts. The only champagne bottle was empty, but she didn't like to make a fuss. She eyed the array of spirits available and her stomach clenched as a terrible doubt gripped her. What on earth would Rick prefer to drink? The only alcohol she knew he liked for sure was red wine, but there didn't seem to be any on offer. She opted for a Scotch for Rick and a gin and tonic for herself.

At the centre of a small gathering across the room, Cynthia was telling some enormously funny joke. People were hooting with laughter. And Cynthia was so overcome with her own wonderful wit that she had to cling to Rick while she screeched uproariously.

Maddy carried the two glasses across the room, desperately hoping her lack of knowledge about her lover's habits would not be exposed within the first five minutes of the party. 'That must have been a good joke,' she said with a smile as she joined the group.

'Too right,' drawled Rick. 'Cynthia's a barrel of laughs.'

Maddy offered him the Scotch.

He took it and frowned. 'What's this?'

With a hopeful little smile, she told him, 'Scotch on the rocks.' But she winced at the look of distaste that flashed across his features.

And, Maddy noted with a sinking heart, sharp-eyed Cynthia was staring at them suspiciously. 'O-oh, for heaven's sake, did I give you the Scotch?' she stammered. 'Sorry, Rick. Here's your gin and tonic. The Scotch is mine, of course.'

There was a fumbled exchange of glasses. 'Thanks, sweetheart,' murmured Rick, and Maddy was sent into a complete tailspin by the gentle way he suddenly looked at her.

'We've realised who you are of course, Rick,' pouted Cynthia. 'Why didn't you tell us you were a television celebrity?'

There was a murmur of excitement and fuss.

A beaming redhead in peacock-blue sequins gazed in adoration at Rick. 'I met another man from television at a party and he was such a disappointment. He was so tiny. But you look even bigger in real life than you do on the screen.'

Rick smiled politely back at the woman and she batted her eyelashes and preened herself self-consciously.

It occurred to Maddy that Rick must be used to being mobbed by women at parties. No wonder he considered this exercise a boring chore—just another job.

'Poor little Maddy,' Cynthia clucked. 'How are you going to cope when your man's away being a busy foreign correspondent so much of the time?'

Maddy felt Rick's fingers gently tugging at one of her curls as he moved close beside her once more. She drew courage from his reassuring presence. 'It doesn't really bother me. And that's the way it is for us thoroughly modern women, isn't it?' she challenged Cynthia. 'We don't want to hold our men back... I certainly won't be sitting at home planning a white dress that looks good from the rear view.'

She glanced quickly at Rick and was surprised to see his sudden frown.

'But it will be hideous for you not knowing what this naughty fellow is getting up to on the other side of the world.'

'Cynthia...' Rick leaned forward quickly, his tone low and coated with velvet menace. 'I would advise you not to judge everybody else by your own dubious standards.'

The smug smirk vanished. Self-consciously, Cynthia's eyes darted around the group, checking to see if anybody else had heard Rick's comment, but the others were holding an impromptu discussion about one of his documentaries and didn't seem to have noticed the exchange. She resurrected a forced smile and spoke brightly. 'Now, everyone, don't forget to enjoy yourself. I must find Byron.'

'He's getting another drink,' another guest told her. 'From what I've seen, you might need to get him to slow down, Cynthia.'

At that, Cynthia drifted unhappily away.

Maddy looked across to where Byron was helping himself at the drinks table. He was staring at her and she was very surprised that she felt no tug of emotion. Her feelings for him had been slipping away for weeks now, but until that moment she hadn't realised just how far she'd come. Surely she must have forgotten just how slim and pale he was? Perhaps it was just the drink, but there was a limp quality about his bearing that she'd never noticed before.

'Now, *we* should put these drinks down and go and dance,' Rick suggested as he took Maddy's untouched glass. 'I take it you don't like Scotch either?'

Smiling, she shook her head.

'Let's go, then,' he said. 'I can hear music out on the deck and the atmosphere's getting a little stuffy in here.'

Gladly, she followed him through the French doors which led to the side deck. Strung with coloured paper lanterns, the area looked rather pretty in the moonlight. Several couples were dancing to a slow, popular number.

But rather than dancing straight away Rick led Maddy to a shadowy corner.

'OK. I need to know a little more about you,' he said quietly.

Maddy stared at him, wondering what on earth had prompted the request. 'Really?' she responded in surprise. 'So you can keep up our pretence more effectively?'

In the moonlight, Rick's eyes smiled down at her. 'Yeah... I guess that's a good enough reason.'

'What—what would you like to know?'

Rick leant back against the deck's railing. 'If you had married Byron, would you have kept on working in the shop?'

'For sure,' she answered without hesitation. Then she looked at him sharply. 'Byron had big plans for expansion. He could see me owning a string of Floral Fantasies—making him a fortune.'

'Is that what you wanted?'

'No!' Maddy frowned as she thought about it. 'I wasn't keen to get caught up in high-powered business. I know it sounds disgustingly old-fashioned of me, but if I—if I—' she took a deep breath. Suddenly, standing in the moonlight with Rick, she felt self-conscious talking about her personal dreams. 'If I ever get married, I want to find a manager, someone like my assistant Chrissie, who'll mind the shop while I stay home and play with my babies.'

She saw Rick's throat work. He glanced at her sharply then quickly shifted his gaze to a distant spot in the garden.

'What about you, Rick? Do you plan to keep dashing around the world?'

He sighed, as if he felt suddenly very weary. 'I can't imagine doing anything else,' he said softly. Then he straightened quickly. 'But let's not get ourselves too tangled up in the future when we have the moon and the starlight, and great music. Let's dance.'

He drew her towards him and suddenly Maddy's legs were trembling again.

'You really are doing quite a good job of pretending,' she whispered.

His eyes gently mocked her. 'This is going to be the hardest part.' Then his arms held her close and as she felt the warmth of his chest meet hers Maddy's heart stood still.

To be in Rick's arms...to feel every line of that strong, sexy body against hers...

He steered her with effortless grace into the middle of the deck, and the rest followed with breathtaking ease. His lips caressed her hair and, with firm, confident control, he held her against him so that her breasts moulded to his chest and his thighs pressed close to her. His hand at the base of her spine applied subtle pressure to her hips. Within minutes, Maddy was on fire.

Every pore of her skin tingled with sensitive awareness of Rick's body, moving slowly, rhythmically, smoothly against hers.

She could smell his clean shirt and something indefinably sexy and male. Was it aftershave? She wasn't sure, but as she rested her head against his shoulder she was very aware of the smooth brown column of his neck above its neat white collar. She wondered how his skin would taste.

He changed position slightly and held her even closer. And she could tell he was as tense as she was. She could feel the force of his masculine need and it took her completely by surprise.

Perhaps we've taken this pretence too far, she thought. Acting as if we are lovers—behaving like lovers. Naturally physical reactions have taken over that have nothing to do with love at all.

The only sensible approach was to keep reminding herself that as soon as this party was over Rick would disappear again. Clear out of her life. But she wanted so badly to push the thought aside. This temporary bliss was too wonderful to analyse. She knew it couldn't possibly be love, but it was something just as good.

'Thanks for letting me borrow you again, Rick.'

Shortly after midnight, Rick and Maddy walked back from the car park towards her shop. 'You convinced everyone at the party that you were my boyfriend—especially Cynthia and Byron. You left no one in doubt about that.'

'It was my pleasure,' Rick drawled. 'Just between you and me, I think Byron is finding being engaged to Cynthia a bit like tying himself to an avalanche.'

'I'm not too worried about how he feels,' replied Maddy. It was true, she realised with a burst of relief. By the end of the evening, all her tender feelings for Byron had drained completely away—like used bath water down a plug hole. She added with a cheeky little grin, 'Did you see Cynthia's expression when we were dancing?'

Rick chuckled briefly. 'I was reassured to discover that many of your other friends are much nicer.'

'Of course they are. I have quite discerning taste most of the time.' She shot him an admiring glance. 'You were the hit of the party.'

Two blocks away, traffic still streamed through the inner city. High above them, the moon hovered over a nearby high-rise apartment.

By the light of a neon sign, Maddy studied Rick. She fancied she saw his jaw clench tightly as he drew in his breath with a sharp hiss. And she wondered, with a stab of alarm, what would happen now. Was he glad to get an annoying chore out of the way? Would they exchange a polite goodnight?

They were neighbours, nothing more, she reminded herself. Rick certainly wasn't looking for a meaningful relationship. He'd grudgingly accompanied her to the party this evening as a special favour. And she certainly didn't want to become involved with another man hot on the heels of her disastrous engagement to Byron. But if this was true, why did she feel such an intense longing to throw herself into Rick's arms? She'd never felt so powerfully attracted to a man. She knew that if he showed the slightest sign of interest in her she would be quite shamelessly overjoyed.

His voice cut into her thoughts. 'It's a pity that I can only lend myself out for this all too brief evening,' he said carefully.

There's your reality check. With a jolt of disappointment, Maddy reproached herself as she continued walking in silence beside him. *Time to stop dreaming. Right now.*

'You know that's how it's got to be, Maddy, don't you? You realise we can't progress with this?' Rick's eyes were fixed intently on her as he spoke. 'In a way, Cynthia hit on the truth. My job doesn't leave much space for romantic relationships.'

'Yes, I understand that, Rick,' she said quickly, not looking at him, and she walked a little ahead of him, in her high-heeled sandals, her hips swaying rhythmically, her head high and shoulders straight.

She closed her eyes and tried to banish the memory of dancing in his arms, his body moving sensuously against hers, thigh to thigh, his strong arms holding her close and his lips in her hair.

They reached the small vestibule beside her shop. Ahead of them was the door to Maddy's flat and to the right the stairs leading to Rick's.

'I totally understand that you want to be a professional bachelor,' she told him. She stared at Rick in the darkness and she fancied she saw his lips curl into the briefest of smiles.

Silence filled the space around and between them.

'That's been my plan,' he muttered eventually.

Maddy shrugged ever so slightly and her keys jangled in her hand as she turned towards her door. 'I really appreciate the enormous effort you made to be here for tonight,' she said, hoping her voice didn't sound too wistful.

Rick stood, watching her in silence as she fitted the key to the lock. 'Maddy!'

She spun around very quickly, her heart suddenly leaping to a hectic tempo. 'Yes?'

And then he didn't seem to know what he wanted to say.

'Know something?' he said at last. 'I seem to be getting very good at lying.'

'Lying?' She left the key dangling in the lock as she faced him. 'You mean pretending all night to be my lov—um—boyfriend?'

'No. I actually meant I was lying before we even left for that party. I said I was calm.'

'And you weren't?' Maddy asked, her eyes wide with surprise. 'No millponds?'

'A cyclone might be more correct. I've felt calmer caught up in a mob of starving rioters. Of course I was nervous at the thought of spending all night pretending to be your regular, live-in lover when I knew damn well it was a sham.'

Despite the chaotic thumping in her chest, Maddy managed another casual shrug as she pushed her door open. 'I knew you weren't as cool as you made out,' she replied, forcing her voice to sound more amused than she felt.

Then, emboldened by some secret force within her, she stepped forward, out of the lamplight, into the warm darkness that lay between them. 'Rick.'

The last faint hint of his aftershave drifted to her.

Rick swallowed and his eyes pierced her with a sharp, glittering fire. 'You should keep walking away from me,' he whispered.

Not knowing at all where she drew her courage from, Maddy placed a shaking finger on his lips. 'I think you deserve a goodnight kiss.'

'Oh, Maddy,' he groaned, pulling her into his arms, and she melted against him. His warm, sensitive lips were temptingly close to hers. 'Your kisses are dangerous.'

'But you like living dangerously.'

'I do indeed.' He cupped her face with both hands, and, as his mouth met hers, Maddy's lips parted to receive his tongue. A shaft of hot desire flared through her. She was sure Rick shared the sensation. It seemed as if his mouth was telling hers of his desperate need.

His lips found her ear. Then her neck. And she had no idea how she did it, but with the slightest delicate movement of her shoulder the tiny strap of pink silk was gone, leaving her shoulder bare and creamy, waiting to be kissed.

Rick's face broke into a broad grin. 'That was clever. Can you do it on the other side as well?'

'I don't know,' she purred, moving softly against him.

There was nothing for it but for Rick to kiss her other ear and the curve of her neck on the other side. And as Maddy wriggled against him the strap fell away.

'Maddy,' he growled, tracing the outline of her collarbone with a shaking hand. 'Now how does your dress stay up?'

She took his hand in hers and pulled him gently through her doorway. 'You journalists ask far too many questions,' she told him with a slow smile.

Church bells—the peals of inner-city cathedrals—woke her. Maddy rolled over, grateful that it was Sunday and that she didn't have to rush into the shop to begin work. She reached over to Rick.

He was gone.

His side of the bed was quite cold as if he'd left it ages ago. Sitting up, Maddy listened carefully to see if she could hear him moving around in the flat—making coffee in the kitchen. But she heard nothing except the muffled sound of traffic outside. Maybe he was sprawled on her sofa quietly reading the paper?

At the thought of finding him absorbed in the news of the world, Maddy smiled and, slipping on an oversized T-shirt, she padded out into the lounge room. It was empty. And so were the kitchen and the bathroom. Her flat was empty and Rick was gone.

She sat down abruptly on the sofa and blinked back sudden, unwanted tears. Don't you dare cry, you idiot! she scolded herself. This is reality! He tried to warn you. This is exactly what you get for pretending to be a sex kitten.

You get sex, but that's all you get!

Memories of her happiness a few short hours earlier mocked her. When Rick had made love to her, there had been a wonderful sense of rightness. Nothing she'd ever experienced before could have prepared her for that. Not the desperate fumblings of her early boyfriends, and certainly not Byron's rather selfish approach to sex. Rick had filled her with joy, excited her beyond dreaming, strengthened her and made her feel totally secure.

She was quite certain she was in love.

But a worldly-wise teenager could have told her that going to bed with a fellow rarely meant he loved you back. Her experience with Byron should have hammered that message home loud and clear. What kind of lame brain was she?

'But he acted like he really cared!' she whispered to the empty room.

Give up! Maddy's common-sense lectured. If she was honest, she should admit that Rick's tenderness and the way he'd gazed at her as if he wanted to keep her beside him for ever were simply impressions fuelled by her overactive imagination. She had coloured the experience with her own yearnings.

Hugging a sofa cushion fiercely, Maddy let out a deep groan. There was nothing to be gained by trying to second-guess Rick's deeper feelings. What she really needed to face up to was the bald fact that *she* had fallen head over heels in love with *him*. Surely there were classes for people like her—remedial classes for romantics who continually fell for the wrong man?

Hadn't he tried to warn her? He'd said they could not progress their relationship and she had ignored that and pushed things to the point of no return.

With another, louder groan, Maddy climbed off the sofa and padded into the kitchen. Usually domestic tasks helped to calm her down. So she set about making some coffee and defrosting croissants for breakfast. While she waited for the coffee to filter, she carefully watered the row of African violets on her windowsill. But she felt no calmer. Her thoughts still boiled. How alarmingly easy it was to fall in love! And, once it had happened, how complicated and difficult it was to switch those feelings off again.

Her microwave pinged and she removed the croissants, placing them on a plate which was part of the special crockery set she reserved for Sunday morning breakfasts—white china decorated with cheerful, hand-painted strawberries.

'Something smells good.'

Maddy jumped and spilt the jam she was spooning onto a croissant.

Rick came striding into the room freshly showered and dressed in jeans and a white T-shirt. A slogan was scrawled in Arabic across his chest and a small canvas backpack was slung casually over one shoulder.

Her eyes feasted on him but her heart jerked painfully. 'You're still here?'

He smiled. 'Last time I checked.'

With a blush of embarrassment, Maddy cursed her habit of stating the obvious. Her blush deepened as she remembered that she'd sprung out of bed without even brushing her hair. Her face would still be smudged with sleep and she wore nothing but a thin T-shirt over a naked body that was tender from Rick's zealous lovemaking.

'Hungry?' she asked, as nonchalantly as she could manage, while she popped one of the croissants onto another plate and reached for a second mug.

'Sure.'

Looking up, she found Rick's gaze resting on her, his grey eyes revealing briefly a perplexing blend of desire and a regret that somehow frightened her. Not knowing what to say, she handed him the plate. They walked to her dining table and she sat down very primly, only too aware of her skimpy clothing.

After her abandoned behaviour last night, it seemed silly to become suddenly modest, but, in the bright light of day, Maddy felt decidedly unsure of herself. Especially as Rick seemed to be returning to his 'polite neighbour' mode—keeping his distance.

He was probably regretting his dalliance with her.

She watched his perfect teeth bite into the croissant as she poured his coffee. Best not to look at his mouth. Not after the intimate way it had explored her body last night. She shifted her gaze to his backpack on the floor beside him.

'So you're off again?' Maddy tried her level best to keep any hint of criticism from her voice.

'I promised my mother I would spend some time with her,' he said.

'That's nice.'

He smiled again and Maddy winced to hear herself sounding so formal.

'She lives on a small property out in the Brisbane Valley—not far from Somerset Dam,' he told her.

'Only about an hour's drive from here,' Maddy commented.

'Yes. I'm not exactly in her good books for taking so long to get out there. My father died some years ago and I'm the only child, so I should make more of an effort. I've promised her at least a fortnight now that Sam's better. After that, there are several assignments lining up.'

Maddy nodded and concentrated on cutting her croissant into tiny pieces as she assimilated this news. Sam was better and Rick was leaving. To his mother's first of all, but then, naturally, he'd be back to work—globetrotting—saving the world.

Forgetting her.

Rick watched her operation in silence for some time. As her thoughts whirled, she couldn't look at him, couldn't speak. She kept cutting the pastry into tinier and tinier pieces. Finally his brown hand reached across the table and closed over hers. She had to stop cutting, but she kept staring at her plate.

'You're a wonderful girl, Maddy,' he said. Then he let her hand go as he thumped the table and sighed harshly. 'Hell—that sounded a damn sight more insipid than I wanted it to.'

Maddy felt a wave of sympathy for him. She'd blatantly lured this man into making love to her and, being a normal, healthy and unattached male, he'd responded with predictable enthusiasm. But now he felt compelled to say something to set things straight without hurting her.

'Rick,' she said quickly before she lost her courage, 'it's OK. I understand.'

A sequence of conflicting emotions flickered across his features—a frown, a half smile and then another, deeper frown. 'You do?'

'Of course,' she responded, forcing her brightest smile. 'You're a nomad. You don't take kindly to being tethered. And besides, you have a string of missions to fulfil. You would prefer to forget last night ever happened. Or, if you do think of it, it should just be as a— a pleasant interlude. Nothing that would tie you to me in any way.'

The furrows on his brow smoothed and he took a deep sip of coffee. 'Even if I did settle down, I would be poor company,' he said softly. 'Racing off from one assignment to another, always getting itchy feet—always finding some new issue or cause to champion.'

'And that's all *I* am to you, really, isn't it?' Maddy

blurted out. But she was immediately embarrassed by her impulsive retort. Lord! She had been trying so hard to be strong. The last thing she wanted was to sound clinging. She toyed with her coffee spoon.

'How do you mean?' Rick asked cautiously.

There was really no choice but to try to explain what she meant. 'I—I think you see me as some kind of underdog who needs support—a worthy cause. I needed rescuing from Cynthia and Byron and like Prince Valiant you came racing back across the oceans to rescue the fair maiden in her distress.' She paused and shot him a challenging look from beneath dark lashes. 'But now it's time to move on to some higher challenge.'

'Maddy! For Pete's sake! I think you're making a mountain out of a molehill.' Rick was staring at her, clearly puzzled, his eyes narrowed as he appraised her. 'We had a deal, sure. But I don't see you as some kind of poor little charity case.'

She held his gaze while her heart pounded loudly in her ears. Rick looked away and shook his head slowly.

And Maddy took the chance to get to her feet and walk across the room. Staring out of a small window at the brick wall of the building next to hers, she stood with her back to him. She took a deep, cleansing breath and spoke as steadily as she could. 'OK, forget that,' she said over her shoulder, although privately she was sure she'd hit on the truth. 'I sounded very ungrateful. I'm sorry. What I meant to say, Rick, is that I appreciate how much you've helped me, but I understand how you feel. You've done your neighbourly good deed and now you're free to move on. I've absolutely no intention of tying you down just because of one—one little—fling.'

He would never know how much it had cost her to say that, but Maddy was proud of herself. She was now a woman of the world! She had behaved like any other modern girl—had a brief affair with a gorgeous guy then waved him off without a whimper.

When Rick didn't reply, she turned around, her chin thrust forward to keep her bottom lip steady. He was staring at her, nodding slowly, thoughtfully.

Standing abruptly, he crossed the room towards her. Maddy held her breath as his hands clasped her shoulders. 'It really was the most delectable of flings, Maddy,' he told her gently. He threaded a finger into one of her long curls and stood staring at it in silence as if searching for the right thing to say.

But she knew there was no comfort he could offer her. Blinking fiercely, Maddy squirmed out of his grasp and hurried to the kitchen. 'L-look at the time,' she stammered, staring at the clock and not seeing what hour it was at all. 'Your mother is expecting you and I—I have all sorts of things to do,' she finished lamely.

She was grateful that he didn't try to kiss her goodbye. He picked up his backpack, swung it over his shoulder and smiled. ''I'll be off, then.'

'I'll look out for you on television,' Maddy offered lightly. 'It'll be fun to say I know someone famous.'

Rick smiled again—a polite, distant smile. He'd probably had that said to him so many times, Maddy thought.

She didn't follow him to her front door. Standing at her kitchen doorway, she watched Rick cross the room and let himself out of her flat.

Out of her life.

CHAPTER SIX

WHEN the phone rang a week later, Maddy was arranging a colourful collection of Australian wild flowers, while trying to stop her thoughts from drifting back once more to Rick with his slow smile, his sensuous touch and his strong, all-male body.

She grabbed the receiver and answered automatically. 'Floral Fantasies, Maddy speaking.'

'I need help with a fantasy,' an all-male voice replied.

Surely it couldn't be.

'Is that Rick?' she asked tentatively.

'How are you, Maddy?' His voice was beautiful—deep and resonant.

'I—I'm just great,' she replied, hoping she didn't sound too breathless. 'Where are you?' Maddy half expected him to be ringing from Beirut or Timbuktu.

'I'm still out at Torrington, my mother's farm.'

'I see. And—and you say you're fresh out of fantasies?'

'I am indeed.' Rick paused. 'What are you doing?' he asked, his voice suddenly low and edgy.

'You mean right now?'

'Yeah.'

Maddy waggled a hand in the air behind her, feeling for a stool to sit on. Her legs were in danger of giving way. 'I-I'm arranging flowers. What would you expect?'

'Are you wearing something pink?'

Oh, Lord! Surely she was imagining that sexy longing in his voice? It was tempting to play along with Rick and to offer some light-hearted, suggestive response. But after a week of forcing herself to be strong and to accept that they had no future together, Maddy knew she couldn't afford to start playing games with him. 'Rick, you sound different. Are you all right?'

'I am now—talking to you.'

She wanted to warn him. *Don't do this to me, Rick. Don't flirt with me. I care too much.* But she had too much pride to admit that.

'So what kind of fantasy are we talking about?' she asked guardedly.

'I'm hoping you'll come with me to the Media Ball on Friday of next week.'

Maddy clutched the phone with both hands. By reaching with her foot, she had finally managed to haul the stool close and she sank gratefully onto it. She was shaking from head to toe.

'Are you there, Maddy?'

A sudden fantasy of her own danced before her eyes—a picture of herself in a dazzling designer gown, sailing on Rick's arm past photographers and celebrities as they entered through the doors of a prestigious hotel and into a glittering ballroom.

This invitation meant that she would be able to dine and dance with Rick again. For a whole evening. And afterwards... The thought of afterwards drenched her with perspiration and an overload of sweet, tantalising memories.

Think of the morning after! It was silly to even let herself contemplate such a date without thinking of the agony of saying goodbye all over again. Maddy sighed. She knew very well that another 'fling' before Rick took off on his next assignment would break her heart completely.

She almost groaned aloud. 'I'm actually very busy next week, Rick.' It was only partly the truth.

After several long seconds, she finally heard his reply. 'One good turn deserves another, you know, Maddy. I escorted you last weekend.'

Maddy drew in a deep, shuddering breath. Did Rick realise he was using emotional blackmail? The price she would pay for another evening with him would be too high. 'I'm sorry, Rick. It would be lovely, but I have Cynthia and Byron's wedding next Saturday. And there's a twenty-first party on the Friday evening. I'm going to be flat out.' She refrained from adding, And Brisbane is full of young women who would love to help you out.

On the other end of the line, she heard Rick's sigh. 'That's a pity.'

'It is,' she said softly, and was so glad he couldn't see her face. She was sure her disappointment would be all too evident. 'But it can't be helped.'

'Of course not,' he said after a silence so long and uncomfortable that Maddy almost changed her mind. He sighed. 'OK, then. Give my regards to the happy couple.'

'I will, Rick. Bye.'

On the following Saturday afternoon, Maddy delivered the boxes of orchid bouquets to Cynthia Graham's home. The bride was still at the hairdresser's. Mrs Graham looked very distracted and flustered when she answered her knock, so Maddy handed over the boxes, gave a few simple instructions and, after passing on her best wishes, left again quite quickly.

While she no longer felt even a twinge of regret about Byron and Cynthia's wedding, she was happy that she didn't have to get too involved. Cynthia had never failed to find a way to annoy Maddy and she was quite certain that even on her wedding day the bride would have something niggling to say.

So it was with a sense of relief that Maddy let herself back into the shop. Other flowers had been sent to the church. The reception rooms were finished. All she had to do now was clean up the back room where stems, leaves, broken flowers, pieces of ribbon and empty buckets still needed to be cleared away.

When the phone rang, Maddy had her arms full of rubbish, so she dumped it first before answering. 'Floral Fantasies.'

'Oh, Maddy. I'm so glad you're still there. For a minute I thought I'd missed you.'

'Is that Cynthia? Is everything all right?'

'You mean the bouquets? Oh, yes, I think so, although I haven't had a chance to look at them yet. I've only just got back from The Hair Affair.'

'Oh. So how can I help you?'

Cynthia's voice lowered. 'I just wanted to make sure that you were OK.'

Puzzled, Maddy frowned as she answered. 'I—I'm perfectly fine, thank you.'

'Oh, that's good. I'm so relieved.'

Maddy was astounded that Cynthia would have an attack of guilty conscience at this late stage. 'I really am very happy for you and Byron,' she told the other woman. 'I hope you have a wonderful wedding.'

'And you don't mind about Rick?' Cynthia's voice was sugar-coated.

'R-Rick?' Maddy closed her eyes. She had been trying so hard not to think about Rick. Last night, while he'd attended the Media Ball, she'd taken herself off to the movies. She'd chosen a particularly gruesome psychological thriller in the hope that it would distract her completely from thinking about him. A foolish hope.

'I don't know what you mean,' she told Cynthia. 'Why should I mind about Rick?'

The sound of Cynthia's silly little laugh as it tinkled down the line was as welcome as the crash of breaking glass.

'Well, my dear girl,' Cynthia gushed, 'I thought Rick was *your* man. I mean he's moved into your flat and, at our party, you sure looked like one smitten kitten.'

Maddy's teeth clenched and her fingers gripped the telephone receiver so tightly they hurt. She didn't want to hear what Cynthia had to say. It could only be something upsetting. Extremely upsetting, probably. If she had any common sense, she would hang up now.

But she couldn't. 'Cynthia,' she almost snarled. 'What are you trying to tell me?'

'You haven't seen this morning's paper, have you?'

Maddy felt dizzy. She swayed against the workbench beside her. Of course she hadn't seen the day's paper. She'd been far too busy getting the flowers ready for this dreadful woman's wedding. But she had a fair idea what had sparked Cynthia's 'concern'.

'Does that paper have a photo from the Media Ball?' she asked, willing her voice not to break. Her eyes darted to her newspaper, still unopened, lying at the end of her front counter.

'It certainly does,' crooned Cynthia. 'Quite an eye-opener. I couldn't believe it.'

Maddy broke in quickly with a forced, brittle laugh. 'Oh, Cynthia, for heaven's sake. A simple photo? Is that all you wanted to tell me? You had me quite worried for a minute.'

'So you didn't mind that Rick went to the ball with Christiana Sloane?'

Christiana Sloane? The long-legged, golden-haired, busty supermodel?

Of course she minded! She minded so badly she wanted to scream. Maddy took a deep breath and forced her face into a grimacing grin as she replied brightly, 'Didn't worry me in the slightest.'

'They looked very *intimate* in the photo.'

With every ounce of her willpower, Maddy sweetened her tone. 'Cynthia, don't you have things to do today?'

'Yes, of course, darling; I'd better go. I'm so pleased to know you're not upset.'

'Thanks for caring,' Maddy purred. 'Hope the morning sickness stays away long enough for you to get through the ceremony.' She dropped the receiver with a crash and stomped across the room.

Cynthia made an art form of bitchiness! Surely the story wouldn't be nearly as suggestive as she had made out? Maddy decided she wouldn't even look at the newspaper. Circling the room like a condemned criminal in a cell, she tried to breathe deeply, to calm down and to think clearly.

But all she could think of was Rick—and how she felt about him! And how she had refused his invitation.

With a cry of despair, Maddy snatched up the newspaper and leafed through the pages frantically. At first she couldn't find what she was looking for. So she spread the paper out on the shop counter and, with shaking hands, turned the pages methodically. And, suddenly, there it was on the social page—a huge photo of Rick looking heartbreakingly handsome in a splendid tuxedo with Christiana Sloane clinging to him like a sucker fish on a shark. The model's slinky dress seemed to dive to below her navel, leaving little of her voluptuous body to the imagination.

'Tough Assignment for Foreign Correspondent', the accompanying caption claimed. Sick and shaking, Maddy scanned the story below. It stated that when the press had quizzed Rick about escorting Christiana he'd joked, 'It's just a job. We're just good friends.'

However, the story went on to give Ms Sloane's version. The model was recovering from a traumatic break-up with her movie stuntman boyfriend and she'd found solace in the arms of the popular TV newsman Rick Lawson.

'As usual,' the story concluded, 'Lawson is playing his cards close to his chest and will not comment on his recent appearance socially with another unnamed beauty.'

Another unnamed beauty? Maddy flinched. It shouldn't surprise her that Rick had a string of beautiful women. She wondered just how recently the other social event had taken place. Miserably she looked again at the photo. Rick's arm encircled Christiana Sloane and his hand curved possessively over her shapely hip. He looked very happy and relaxed.

By contrast, Maddy felt absolutely wretched. She wrapped her arms around her middle to try to ease the sick feeling that had settled in the pit of her stomach.

She tried to convince herself that she didn't care that Rick had spent the night with one of Australia's most beautiful women. Like hell she didn't! Now her brave and sensible gesture of rejecting Rick's invitation made absolutely no sense at all. She had refused the invitation because she hadn't wanted another brief affair, only to have Rick take off again. But if she'd known the alternative was throwing him into the eager arms of Christiana Sloane...!

Maddy cringed at the thought of the supermodel's astonishing beauty. Half the world's richest playboys had pursued that woman.

She paced the shop floor, feeling totally alone. How much of this year was she going to spend feeling so terrible? So defeated? When was she ever going to be able to get on with her life again without worrying about some man? They weren't worth it. First there had been Byron and he had proved to her that she'd wasted far too much energy yearning for him. And pining for Rick made no sense either.

He had no interest in permanent relationships; he was married to his job. He'd made it very clear that he wanted his freedom. And Maddy could easily imagine that a girl like Christiana Sloane would be able to love and leave Rick with the carefree ease that he required.

She had absolutely no idea where Rick was during the miserable weeks that followed. The only contact she had was watching the documentary he'd made about Cambodia. It was screened on television one Friday evening. Throughout the entire program, she sat on the sofa, hugging a cushion and bawling her eyes out.

It was agony to watch him. The way he moved with easy, athletic grace—each gesture, each change in facial expression and even the timbre of his voice were all so familiar that watching him made her eyes stream with hot, burning tears and her throat ache wretchedly.

She knew it was nothing short of idiotic to tape his program so that she could replay it on video and relive the agony over and over. But that was exactly what she did. And the newspapers provided another form of torture for Maddy. There seemed to be an endless stream of photographs of Rick and Christiana Sloane accompanied by suggestive captions.

As far as Maddy could determine, Christiana was accompanying Rick on his travels, or at the very least meeting up with him to rendezvous in various exotic locations.

From Bangkok came a photo of them attending another glittering function. 'Supermodel steps out with Aussie newsman', the headlines claimed. In Tokyo they were dancing—Rick looking dashing in a tuxedo and Christiana in something backless and sleek. The caption, 'Cool Rick warms to Christiana', kept Maddy miserable for days. But the most dreadful blow of all came a fortnight later, when she saw a photo on the celebrity gossip page of a glossy magazine. Rick and Christiana were snapped shopping in Singapore. Dressed in casual clothes, they were laughing together in the most relaxed and intimate of poses, while they selected tropical fruit from a street-market stall. 'Christiana and Rick—inseparable?' asked the magazine.

Maddy stared at the photo with hot, tear-blurred eyes. Christiana was resting her glossy head on Rick's shoulder as they examined the ripeness of rambutans. She knew that she should be happy for Rick. He was wise to seek the companionship of a woman who had a similar outlook. And it seemed he had found someone beautiful and sexy, who could share his lifestyle. Christiana would have no problems leading a chaotic, jet-setting life. She would probably shriek with horror at the thought of settling down and having a family—the kind of humble stuff Maddy's dreams were made of.

* * *

Several miserable weeks later, at six o'clock on an early Monday morning, Maddy drove back from the markets filled with a new resolve to get on with her life once more. She dumped her purchases in the shop, showered and dressed and headed straight to her collection of video tapes. It took mere seconds to find the one marked 'Spotlight on Asia' and to march with it to the garbage bin in the alley behind her shop. There she flung it into the pile of rubbish, slammed the lid down and strode back into her kitchen to eat a hearty breakfast.

That was the end of Rick Lawson.

She felt empty, but at least she wasn't weighed down anymore by an overwhelming sense of longing. She'd let him go. He could have Christiana. She was a new woman.

After a glass of freshly squeezed orange juice, two hot and buttery blueberry muffins and a fresh fruit salad, Maddy realised she'd spent a little too long on her hearty breakfast and so she carried her coffee mug through to the shop to begin organising her business for the day.

The first customer came through the shop door just as she downed the last dregs of the cooling brew. A tall, elderly woman with stylishly cut silver hair entered and paused, looking around her at the floral displays.

'Hello,' Maddy responded, cheerily confident. 'Can I help you?'

'I see this is Floral Fantasies, so you must be Madeline Delancy,' the woman said with a warm smile.

'I am indeed,' Maddy replied with an answering smile. She wasn't sure if it was simply her determination to be optimistic, but she had good vibes about this caller and out of the corner of her eye checked that her order book and a pencil were within reach on the counter.

'You're here bright and early,' she told the customer. 'I don't have everything out on display yet.'

'That's all right, Madeline,' the woman said. 'I don't want to buy any flowers today, but I would like to place an order for a wedding.'

'Oh, lovely.' Maddy turned to the shelf behind her. 'I have albums of photos with examples of the kinds of arrangements I can provide.'

'I want something fairly traditional and simple, really,' the woman explained. 'It's to be a country wedding on my farm—a little way out of the city limits. Would it still be possible for you to help me?'

Maddy loved country weddings. Once upon a fanciful time she'd planned one of her own. She'd never actually provided flowers outside the Brisbane district, but if this place wasn't too far away it could be just the kind of distraction she needed. Something different. A new business challenge.

The woman was watching her with hopeful grey eyes as Maddy considered her request.

'Can you give me a few more details?' Maddy asked as she opened her diary. 'I need to check the date and just how far out you are and I'd like a general idea of the quantities and types of flowers you require.'

The woman happily explained her situation and the good vibes Maddy had sensed when she'd first come into the shop strengthened. There was something reassuring and comfortable about this customer. They examined the albums and chatted happily for some time. Maddy knew it was going to be a pleasure to deal with her. She decided to accept the order. 'I can manage that,' she told her. 'Now let me just take down those details for your order.'

As Maddy completed the list, the woman beamed.

'This will be wonderful,' she told Maddy warmly. 'I'm so pleased. I do so want this to be a pretty wedding and my son has told me so much about your lovely flower arrangements. He insisted I try you first.'

'Really?' Maddy responded, and frowned as she studied the good-looking, grey-eyed woman before her. She realised she hadn't yet written her name at the top of the order form. 'So I know your son? I—I'm sorry,' she stammered. 'I didn't catch your name.'

'Helen Lawson, my dear.'

As the hairs on the back of her neck rose, the pencil in Maddy's hand circled wildly on the page, but she didn't even notice she was doodling. 'Helen Lawson,' she repeated, and the pencil snapped loudly.

'You know my son, Rick?'

She could still hear Helen Lawson's voice, but Maddy felt as if she'd fallen to the bottom of a well. The voice sounded hollow and echoing, as if it were reaching her from a great distance. What a dingbat! Why hadn't she guessed this was Rick's mother? She lived out in the Brisbane Valley, for heaven's sake. And the woman was good-looking, well spoken and had the same lively grey eyes as Rick.

Rick was getting married!

Maddy felt hot and sweaty. Sick. Her hand clutched her chest. Oh, Lord, this was awful. This was bizarre! Why on earth had she agreed to do this job before she had even found out whom she was dealing with? 'Thank you, Mrs Lawson,' she whispered.

'Thank *you*, Madeline,' Helen Lawson replied. She reached into her handbag. 'Now, here's a sketch map to help you find us. Rick is going to be so pleased I managed to persuade you to take on this job.'

Maddy nodded wordlessly and forced a bleak smile.

Rick's mother closed her handbag and looked ready to depart.

'So how is Rick?' Maddy burst out.

'Oh, he's fine, my dear. Still in Singapore at the moment. You know what he's like—never in the one spot for very long. I don't know how he'll take to settling down when the time comes.'

When the time comes!

She would not give in to the overwhelming temptation to ask about what particular *time* Helen Lawson was referring to. But it had to be his wedding. And she had absolutely no doubt who the bride would be. Christiana Sloane for sure!

As Rick's mother left the shop, Maddy let out a loud groan. This was impossible. Just half an hour ago, she'd vowed to put Rick Lawson out of her mind. To forget about him completely and to get on with her life. *And now she was providing flowers for his wedding!*

She slumped across the counter, her head in her hands. Surely this kind of cruel twist of fate didn't happen twice in one girl's life? Was she doomed to spend her days decorating weddings for former lovers? How much bad luck was she expected to bear? She hadn't broken any mirrors lately.

That it was Rick's wedding was horribly, painfully clear. He had told Maddy he was an only child—the only son his mother could be referring to. And Mrs Lawson was going to so much trouble to have things the way he wanted them.

She was surprised that Christiana Sloane would be content with a simple country wedding, but, she reminded herself wretchedly, sometimes celebrities liked to get out of the limelight and they enjoyed cosy, intimate celebrations with just a few special friends and relatives. And country weddings were still trendy.

Elbows propped on the counter, she reflected that life really wasn't fair. She'd started this day so confidently. And now she felt like a foolish fish that had swallowed the bait—hook, line and sinker. Surely she'd been bitten once, and she should have been doubly shy the second time? How had this nightmare happened?

Dragging buckets of flowers out of the back storeroom, Maddy continued to set up the shop's display. Without enthusiasm she arranged brightly mixed bouquets near the shop's entrance. Her mind tussled with her dilemma as she worked. She was hugely disappointed with Rick.

Disappointed? She was mortified! Rick had asked his mother to engage Maddy. After he had claimed to be disgusted by Byron's cavalier treatment of her, he was treating her just as badly.

And this time it hurt so much more.

She placed an enormous assembly of blue irises just near the front counter and immediately memories of the first day she'd met him crowded in. She could see him again in her mind's eye, dashing into the shop when the stepladder wobbled. Huge tears welled in her eyes and spilled out over her cheeks.

But her sobs hiccuped to a halt as a new and terrible thought hit her.

She had no right to be so upset!

There had never been any suggestion that she and Rick would ever be more than friends.

They'd had one brief fling.

Maddy repeated the harrowing truth to herself as she sorted price tags. *One brief fling!* Too bad it felt like so much more. Her soppy romantic dreaming had taken over once again and she'd blown up a chance affair into grand love.

Rick was not her fiancé. Had never come close. And here she was crying bucketloads as if she'd been stranded at the altar! As the bell over the shop door tinkled, indicating another customer, she shook her curls in frustration. *Get a grip, girl!*

Maddy didn't feel a whole lot better three weeks later as she headed the Floral Fantasies van out of the western suburbs and into the Brisbane Valley. She was regretting her reluctance to find someone else to do this delivery to the Lawson wedding. She wasn't a masochist—had never enjoyed pain. And this was certainly going to hurt.

Sighing, she turned onto the highway. Deep down she knew why she was doing this. Rick had encouraged her to prove to Cynthia and Byron that she wasn't hurting by providing the flowers for their wedding, and now she would do the same for his. He'd urged her to rise above them. And so she had to do some more rising—above Rick and his bride.

'I'm not a piece of yeast,' she yelled at an innocent cow as her van dashed past. But, nevertheless, she knew she would rise to the occasion once more. She would show Rick just how strong she was.

Or die in the attempt.

As the little van bumped up the track to the farmhouse, Maddy could see Rick hurrying across the verandah and down the front steps. With her teeth clenched tightly together, she jumped out of the driver's seat and opened the doors at the back of the van.

'Hey there,' he called as he hurried over to her. 'Long time no see.'

She whirled around as if he'd startled her. 'Hello, Rick.' Her voice was flat, without emotion.

'How are you?' he asked cheerily.

Maddy stared at him coldly before turning back to the van. She wouldn't let herself think about how gorgeous he looked in old jeans and a faded denim shirt. 'Where do you want these?' she asked, indicating with a sweep of her hand the vast quantities of flowers inside.

'On the side verandah,' Rick told her. And she could tell that he was surprised by her distant manner. Too bad; he'd dealt her a few surprises of his own lately.

'Here, let me help.' He laid a hand lightly on her arm and his eyebrow lifted sharply when she flinched.

'You go inside and get ready, Rick,' Maddy almost snapped. 'I'm sure you have heaps to do. I can manage these. How do you think I got them into the van in the first place?'

Rick stepped back, eyeing her thoughtfully. 'Is something wrong, Maddy?'

'What makes you think that?'

He rumpled his hair with his fingers. 'Forgive me if I'm mistaken, but you seem especially prickly. And—you don't look well. I mean you're just as beautiful as ever,' he quickly corrected, 'but have you lost weight?'

'I might have,' she sniffed. What was it to him?

'Let me help you anyway,' he smiled, using his most placating tone. 'I'm at a bit of a loose end until the ceremony starts.'

Maddy dumped a huge bunch of red roses with long, thorny stems into his arms. 'At least you'll have plenty to do then,' she snapped.

Rick's brow creased in a puzzled frown. 'Pardon?'

She picked up another bunch of roses—white blooms this time—and thrust them roughly towards him. And she shot him a challenging glare. 'Once the ceremony starts you'll be centre stage,' she said.

'Not really,' Rick replied, and grimaced as a bunch of long-stemmed yellow roses headed his way.

Maddy paused, still holding the yellow roses. 'What do you mean, "not really"?' she cried. 'Surely you can't get much more central in a wedding ceremony than being the groom?'

'Groom?' Rick accepted the third bunch of roses gingerly. 'What groom?'

'For crying out loud, Rick,' Maddy shouted, her hands on her hips and her face flushed. 'This is a wedding, right?'

'Sure.'

'*Your* wedding.'

'No.'

'And so, obviously—' Maddy froze and her mouth hung open as she stared at him. Rick watched, fascinated, and she could feel a bright flush creep up her neck and into her cheeks. Her eyes widened 'Not—*not* your wedding?' she gasped.

'No way.' Rick smiled as he shook his head.

She closed her eyes and swayed dizzily as a wave of hot shock engulfed her.

'Hey, careful,' Rick called. He shoved the three bunches of roses onto one arm, so he could reach out to steady her. 'Maddy, you're not well.'

'No, I'm fine, Rick,' she assured him. She smiled shakily. 'Honestly,' she added, letting go of his arm and straightening her shoulders. 'I wasn't feeling too good at the thought of bringing flowers for your wedding—'

'*My* wedding? Good Lord, Maddy. Whatever gave you that idea?'

In answer, Maddy rolled her eyes, shrugged and

turned to drag more flowers from the back of the van. She could list half a dozen news stories and photos that, aided by her seething imagination, had multiplied into hundreds of possibilities. 'We'd better get these out of the heat,' she muttered.

As they walked towards the farmhouse, Rick's questions persisted. 'Why did you think I was getting married? You know I'm allergic to the married state.'

She shot him a wary glance.

He let out his breath in what appeared to be a surge of righteous anger. 'Anyway, how on earth could you think I would pull a dirty stunt like that ex-fiancé of yours?'

Maddy eyed him a little shamefacedly from behind an armful of lilies and greenery. A sudden breeze lifted her dark hair away from her face. She heard the sharp intake of his breath and her own throat tightened at the way he was staring at her.

'I—I guess I jumped to conclusions,' she admitted. Then she paused and squinted at him in the bright sunlight. 'So who *is* getting married?'

Rick's face broke into a broad grin. 'My mother.'

That stumped her. Maddy felt stunned and confused.

Rick looked just as stunned and none too well either. 'You—you haven't been making yourself ill just thinking I was getting married, have you?' he asked in a voice thick with emotion. Then, suddenly, he leaned forward and, heedless of crushing flowers and pricking thorns, curved his hand around her nape, drawing her mouth up to his.

And, without another thought, her mouth welcomed his. After all, it was a kiss she'd been dreaming about for weeks.

When he reluctantly let her go, Maddy knew she was

blushing. For a little longer, he held her chin in his hand, linking her eyes with his, as if he was drinking in every detail of her special brand of beauty.

Her face pulled into an embarrassed smile. 'You're full of surprises, Rick,' she said. Then she broke eye contact and cast a quick professional eye over the flowers. 'No harm done,' she said with a guilty smile. 'So, your mother is getting married?'

'She certainly is. After ten years of widowhood, she's snared an old flame from way back—Jack Hutchins. Come and say hello.'

As Rick led the way onto the verandah, Maddy followed, her heart soaring with an explosion of relief and happiness. Rick wasn't getting married. She felt incredibly light-hearted. It was hard not to grin. Not that it really altered anything about their relationship, she reminded herself. Nothing had changed fundamentally. Rick was still a globetrotter and Christiana wouldn't have vanished into thin air.

Helen Lawson walked towards her, her arms outstretched in welcome. Slightly behind her followed a tall, balding man with a gentle smile.

'Hello, my dear,' Rick's mother greeted Maddy. And, as Rick performed the relatively simple task of introducing Maddy to his future stepfather, Helen Lawson's gaze rested on her son with glowing pride. But then she turned her attention to the flowers.

'Oh, don't these look wonderful?' Her grey eyes sparkled as she examined the flowers and then beamed as they rested on Maddy. 'It's only going to be a tiny wedding, but I did so want it to look pretty. Maddy, thank you so much for going to the trouble of coming all the way out here.'

'It's a pleasure. I needed a change of routine,' Maddy

replied, relieved that she could now make such a claim with genuine enthusiasm.

'You can put them on the trestle table here, Maddy,' Helen instructed. 'My friend from the next property is going to help me transform this old verandah.'

'I'd love to help, too,' Maddy offered, and then suddenly bit her lip as Rick's mother hesitated. Helen Lawson might find such eagerness from a relatively unknown florist rather intrusive.

'That'd be great, Maddy,' Rick said quickly.

'Of course, my dear,' added Helen.

'I have your bouquet and buttonholes in a refrigerator in the back of the van. I'll just fetch them,' she offered. At Helen's nod, Maddy spun around and hurried out to the van.

It was such a sudden turnaround to arrive here expecting to meet Rick's bride and to find instead that he wasn't being married. She needed a quiet moment to collect her thoughts. But as she reached deep into the back of the van, two masculine hands on her hips told her this would not be such a moment.

'Maddy,' she heard Rick say softly, his voice thick with wanting.

She turned and he wrapped his arms around her waist, pinning her to him.

'Rick, your mother is waiting for—'

'No, she isn't,' he muttered huskily. 'She's busy with roses at the moment.' He held her close and she could feel his broad chest pressing against her breasts. She could feel every hard line of his body. And she could feel her own response. Every nerve-ending seemed to be working overtime.

'I need another kiss, Maddy.'

'Another one?' she laughed in breathless surprise.

'That's right.' With his finger, he traced a line down the centre of her forehead, down her nose to her lips. 'I need you. It's been so long.'

Alarm bells rang somewhere in the dim depths of Maddy's consciousness. She *should* mention a certain long-legged, blonde temptress. And even if that wasn't an issue she was supposed to be keeping away from this man. But she'd just spent several miserable weeks avoiding Rick and it hadn't improved her life any. And how could she reason now with his sexy eyes and mouth mere inches from hers?

There could be no harm in one little kiss.

But the instant Rick's mouth sealed with hers Maddy realised that one little kiss could cause a great deal of harm. She had thought she could playfully agree to his demand and then push him away while she continued to collect the rest of the flowers. She could exchange a short, friendly kiss. No worries.

But she hadn't counted on that old magic that seemed to take place whenever she and Rick came together. How did it happen? Two mouths, two bodies met and the rest of the world vanished. Her reality became the circle of Rick's arms.

'Sweet Maddy,' he murmured, briefly lifting his lips from hers and looking down at her from beneath lids heavy with desire.

Heat flared low inside her and his tongue sought hers once more. His hands slid lower, holding her tight against him. Rick, Rick, Rick…she needed him to go on kissing and holding and touching her for ever.

And it seemed he had no plans to let her go. He moved her backwards around to the side of the van, so they couldn't be seen from the house, and his hips pressed her firmly against the metal. She lifted her face and opened her mouth to his, welcoming him.

And as he lowered his lips to hers Rick whispered, 'You'll stay tonight, Maddy, won't you?' He teased her soft lip with his own.

Maddy knew there were plenty of reasons for refusing—several sound and sensible reasons. But she could only think of one.

'Aren't you already spoken for?' she managed to ask, while her heart thrashed around like a frightened bird in a cage. 'The papers are full of your new romance.'

'You mean with Christiana?'

Maddy could have hit him. Who else would she mean?

Rick drew back slightly and his smiling eyes held hers. 'Add another seven centimetres to Cynthia and you have Christiana,' he drawled. 'I think she finally got the hint in Singapore. She's not my type.' He kissed the tip of her nose. 'So what do you think, Maddy? Can I tempt you to stay?'

Maddy suppressed a whoop of joy at his news about Christiana. She tried to remember all the other good reasons for refusing Rick. But all she could think of was that she needed Rick's loving as much as she needed a beating heart. Staying with him was no longer a matter of choice, it was a necessity.

'Your mother won't mind?' she asked.

'I'm thirty-two years old, Maddy. I don't have to ask my mother's permission. I'm asking you. Please stay.' His hips wedged tightly against hers, leaving her in no doubt about his less than honourable intentions.

'How can I refuse when you ask me so nicely?' she replied, shocked by the sultry longing in her voice.

Rick smiled and nuzzled her ear, her jaw. His lips moved over hers...

'Er—excuse me.' Jack Hutchins's embarrassed cough sounded behind them.

Rick looked up. 'Jack?'

'Sorry, mate,' the older man mumbled. 'Helen sent me to see if you needed a hand with bringing anything else in.' He grinned shyly. 'I think I was getting in the way up there.'

Rick sent Maddy a slow, smiling wink as he released her. Flustered, she darted quickly to the open door of the van. 'Let me see, Jack,' she said in her most businesslike voice. 'I have quite a few delicate things here. So a spare pair of hands would be useful.'

She handed out dainty buttonholes, a table centrepiece and Helen's exquisite bouquet and Jack grinned excitedly. 'The last time I got married, I wasn't involved in any of the setting up,' he told them. 'I just turned up on the day and got hitched. It's rather nice to see the whole scenario.'

'Make the most of it,' laughed Rick. 'I think Mum will make sure this is your last wedding.'

Jack grinned. 'I sure hope so.' Then he looked from Rick to Maddy and nodded knowingly. 'Perhaps Helen can start planning your wedding next.'

Maddy held her breath as she sneaked a sideways glance at Rick. She saw him force a smile, although his eyes looked as hard as grey slate.

'I think my mother knows I'm not the marrying kind,' he said quietly.

CHAPTER SEVEN

'I THINK I'm a country person at heart,' Maddy claimed as she perched on the rail of Torrington's front verandah. At the end of the day, she was watching the sun slip down behind the distant range. She admired the beauty of the valley as it stretched before her, bathed in a soft, early evening glow.

Rick stood beside her and his gaze dropped to her slim hands still holding his mother's bouquet in her lap. She was fiddling with the white satin ribbons.

The tossing of the bouquet had been an embarrassing moment. Maddy wondered how deliberately Rick's mother had aimed her throw. When she and Jack were about to leave on their honeymoon, she'd let her bouquet fly and the flowers had virtually landed in Maddy's lap. Everyone had cheered and more than a few of the men had slapped Rick on the back.

She had been forced to lower her eyes to try to hide her confusion. It had taken a few moments before she'd recovered enough to laugh and joke with everyone.

She shrugged the memory aside. 'That was one of the nicest weddings I've ever seen,' she said. 'I loved the informality and your mother looked so very happy. Jack looked pretty pleased with himself, too.'

Rick nodded and gave her hand a little squeeze. 'Thanks for helping out. I don't think anybody expected you to do so much. I hear you were a tower of strength in the kitchen.'

She shrugged and smiled. 'I like doing that kind of thing.'

'Fetching and carrying? Loading dishwashers?' He reached over and pushed a tendril of hair out of her eyes and she turned her cheek to rest it against his hand.

'There are some other activities I prefer,' she murmured seductively, pressing her lips into his palm.

Rick released a heavy sigh and his eyes looked thoughtful. He didn't look at all like a man on the verge of an evening of happy romance. What had happened to the sexy, seductive Rick of this morning? Maddy felt an all too familiar shadow of uncertainty hover in the air between them. Instead of sweeping her into his arms, he patted her cheek in a rather fatherly manner. 'How would you like to see over the property before it's too dark?'

'Oh?' Maddy couldn't hide her surprise. One fine eyebrow arched speculatively. 'Do we have time? How big is this place?'

'Torrington's quite a small holding these days,' Rick replied. 'Mum sold a lot of land after Dad died. Come on, we'll take the truck,' he held out his hand to her and she followed him happily enough, leaving the bridal bouquet on the cane rocker near the front steps.

As they bumped along a rough dirt track, Rick shot a rueful grin at Maddy, bouncing around on the seat beside him. Every so often, the truck would lurch so that she fell against his shoulder. The farm truck was rather battered and rusty and it was difficult to talk over the roar of its ancient motor. 'I'm afraid everything on this place is getting a bit run-down. Mum's kept the house nice, but the rest of the property's slowly reverting to scrub,' he shouted.

'What about Jack?' Maddy asked. 'Does he have plans for the farm?'

Rick shook his head. 'No. Jack's a retired accountant. He wouldn't know one end of a tractor from the other. And I think he's frightened of cattle.'

'That's a pity,' Maddy mused. 'So what are their plans?'

Rick changed to a lower gear as the track descended rather steeply towards a creek bed. 'They're going to travel all over Europe for the next three months. That's Jack's focus now—to travel and to have a good time. He's also been talking about moving into a small apartment in town and I think Mum's happy with that idea, too.'

The vehicle ground its way up the steep track that climbed out of the dry creek bed. 'I'm sure they deserve some fun and fewer responsibilities,' Maddy said as they reached the top of the far bank. She looked thoughtfully out of the truck window. 'But it's a pity about the property. Apart from anything else, it's pretty dry here. We're coming into summer and as far as I can see the firebreaks are all overgrown. This place could be quite a fire hazard if it's just left to revert to nature.'

Rick applied the brake and, as the truck growled to a standstill, he stared at Maddy. 'You're dead right,' he said. 'I hadn't even given bushfires a thought.'

'You're just a pretty face, aren't you?' Maddy teased. 'Honestly, Rick, you need to think about fires. Every summer while I was at uni, I used to do volunteer work with the rural fire brigade in the district around my parents' farm and I've developed a healthy respect for fires. They can be mighty scary and it pays to take precautions.'

Rick's breath expelled in a hiss as his hand slapped

against the steering wheel. 'Damn!' he exclaimed. 'I really should do something. And soon.'

'I don't want to sound too alarmist,' countered Maddy. 'But it is November already. The temperatures will be shooting up from now on.'

Rick nodded silently as he revved the engine once more and pressed his foot to the accelerator.

Maddy suppressed a sigh. For a moment, when he'd first stopped the vehicle, she'd thought Rick was going to take her in his arms and kiss her out here in the twilight. Trust her to divert him with practical concerns like firebreaks. She had obviously squashed his romantic impulses. And now she would have to wait a little longer. Talk about fires! At the thought of the night ahead, she could sense her body heating up for something quite spectacular.

Rick edged the truck along a faint track as they circled back towards the farmhouse. 'I'm off to Hong Kong on Monday,' he informed her. 'That job should only take about two weeks. I know it's cutting things too fine, but I'll just have to pray that we get some November storms to keep the timber damp till I get back then.'

'I can come out on weekends and keep an eye on the place,' Maddy volunteered. She dragged her eyes away from Rick's profile and the sight of his strong, capable hands expertly handling the steering wheel and gear stick, and leaned out of the truck's window to watch the gum trees disappear into the black shadows of encroaching night. Every so often the dancing headlights caught them and momentarily transformed their pale trunks to dazzling silver and as Rick steered the vehicle around a bend she caught sight of a family of wallabies hopping off into the undergrowth. She loved the bush and she would be happy to keep a check on Torrington.

'If you're free to come out and you really want to, that would be great,' Rick told her. 'But I should start thinking about a caretaker. I'm afraid Mum and Jack have been too taken up with each other to pay enough attention to those sorts of matters. They've organised neighbours to keep an eye on the herd and that's about all.'

They reached the house again and Rick parked near the side steps. Maddy jumped down. She could readily sympathise with Helen and Jack's distraction. If they felt half as dizzy as she felt when she was with Rick, just planning a honeymoon would have taken up most of their powers of concentration. But she was a little surprised by their casual attitude. Maddy had always remained practical, no matter how tumultuous her emotional state. She knew from experience that keeping her home and business well organised helped her to retain her sanity when the rest of her life felt as if it was collapsing all around her.

As she followed Rick into the house, her mind tossed over the problem of caring for Torrington. 'The land around here would be quite suitable for crops as well as grazing,' she mused.

Rick turned and smiled down at her, one eyebrow raised in curiosity. 'What are you plotting now, Maddy?'

'A caretaker,' she replied enigmatically.

'You have someone in mind?'

'Perhaps... Can't you guess?'

They reached the kitchen and Maddy moved to the sink to fill the electric kettle. Rick leaned against the kitchen table and crossed his arms over his chest. His eyebrows lowered into a frown. 'Is this a riddle? We have a common acquaintance who would make a suitable caretaker for my mother's farm?'

'We do.'

He shook his head as he sent her a sceptical smile. 'I'm afraid you've beaten me on this one. I don't have a clue.'

'I think Sam might be interested.'

Rick's jaw dropped. 'Sam? Sam Chan? My cameraman?'

Maddy lifted two clean mugs from the dishwasher. 'Well, you know how keen he is to set up a market garden.'

'He is?'

'Like his grandfather's.'

Rick passed his hand over his eyes then scratched his head. 'Sam Chan,' he explained with poorly contained patience, 'is a top television cameraman. He's won awards for his filming around the world. Where on earth did you get the idea he would like to tie himself to a little patch of dirt and grow...' Rick waved his hands in the air helplessly 'and grow...vegetables.'

It was Maddy's turn to fold her arms across her chest. 'He *told* me that's what he wants to do. The accident has given him a chance to rethink his future. He's always had a hankering to run a market garden. And this property is ideally positioned close to Brisbane. It would take a lot of work, but...'

Rick sank onto a chair. 'He told you that? He actually said he's always dreamed of—of growing things?'

She nodded as she spooned instant coffee into their mugs. 'He told me at the hospital.'

'I live and work with the man for ten years, I consider him to be my best mate—and you spend five minutes with him and discover his heart's desire.'

'I wouldn't go so far as to claim that.' Maddy stirred

Rick's coffee and brought it across to him. She placed it on the pine table next to where he sat.

Rick wound his arms around her waist and buried his head against her chest. 'Oh, Maddy, you're a little miracle,' he murmured.

Not knowing what to say, she placed a tentative hand on his head, relishing the soft and silky texture of his hair.

'My mother was right,' Rick said. 'She told me you were very special.'

Maddy laughed, embarrassed. 'I'm not particularly special and I've never been known to achieve miracles. Good grief! You make me sound like a saint.' She lowered herself onto Rick's lap and wriggled against him. 'I can assure you, Rick,' she murmured into his ear, 'there is absolutely nothing saintly about what I'm contemplating.'

Rick grinned and, with his thumb, outlined her lips. 'You're a saintly witch.' Then he groaned. 'All I can think about is making love to you.' He closed his eyes and sighed a deep, throaty sigh.

Maddy leaned forward and touched her lips to each of his closed eyelids in turn.

At last.

She'd been beginning to think they would never get around to lovemaking. 'Good thinking, Mr Lawson,' she murmured huskily. 'We're definitely on the same wavelength.'

She moved her lips lower and Rick clasped her to him as his mouth found hers. He kissed her with the desperation of a condemned man pleading for mercy. His arms wound around her, binding her tightly against him, and his tongue sought to bury itself in the silken recesses of her mouth.

Maddy happily gave herself up to his dominance. This closeness was what she'd been craving all day—ever since she'd discovered Rick wasn't getting married. All afternoon her body had tingled with eager anticipation of what would follow once she and Rick were alone.

While she'd watched Rick's mother exchange her vows with Jack, she'd comforted herself with Sam Chan's reassurances in the hospital. Sam had claimed that Rick was fighting a losing battle over his feelings for her and she was sure Sam was right. Soon, very soon, Rick would give in and acknowledge that he was falling for her.

Rick was unbuttoning her blouse and she moaned with delightful expectation. She needed his intimate touch so badly. 'Let me,' she whispered heatedly. 'I'm faster.'

But as her fingers flew to release the buttons she felt Rick's hand still her action.

'Maddy,' he whispered urgently. 'Maddy, no. Wait. We mustn't. Oh, God!' He groaned and pulled her head against his shoulder. 'Oh, Maddy. What am I going to do with you?'

She felt a cold shiver race up her spine and dart icy fingers around her heart. 'You were doing damn splendid,' she whispered back.

His mouth curled in a half-hearted smile. 'I was being damn selfish,' he told her sadly.

Maddy sat up straighter and stared at Rick. 'Selfish?' she echoed, clearly puzzled. 'I—I don't think so. I get quite a deal of—of pleasure from this kind of behaviour as well, you know.'

His hands framed her face and he let out a short-lived laugh. 'No, Maddy, I'm not talking about being selfish physically. I'm thinking about the long-term scene.'

The icy fingers tightened their grip in the centre of

Maddy's chest and the wonderful evening's happiness vanished. A terrible sense of foreboding filled her and dread settled like a heavy weight in her stomach. There was absolutely no chance that Rick was about to admit that he loved her.

Slipping off his lap, she walked across the room, keeping her back to him as she struggled to suppress suffocating waves of panic. They'd had this kind of conversation before; it shouldn't be so difficult. But when she turned to face him she knew her eyes were extra-wide with the effort to keep tears at bay. 'What exactly are you trying to say, Rick?'

Rick stood up too and began to pace the room, with his hands thrust in his pockets and his head down. 'You deserve so much more than I can offer you, Maddy.'

'What have I asked for?' she cried. 'I'm not demanding. I—I just like—being with you.'

'For now you do,' Rick said softly. 'But what about the future? You deserve so much more, Maddy. You need cosy kitchens and cute little babies tucked up in cradles and a dependable man who will be around to help you decorate the Christmas tree...'

Maddy heard her breath strangle on a choked cry. Heavens! How did Rick know all of these things were exactly what she longed for—what she dreamed of? She wrapped her hands across her middle and stared at him, unable to speak.

He kept pacing and talking. 'Your mission in life is to create a beautiful, cosy nest for some lucky man and to love and nurture him and his children.' He paused and looked at her sadly. 'Am I right?'

She tried to shake her head, to deny his words, but she knew she couldn't deceive Rick. One of the qualities that made him so appealing was the way he understood her so well. Apart from the fact that he could represent Australia in the next kissing Olympics, Rick had always been able to sense her emotions and her needs.

It was why she loved him!

Oh, sweet Lord! Maddy felt her hands fly to her face as the full weight of this truth rushed over her. She loved Rick Lawson with a depth and breadth that was frightening.

He moved across the short space of kitchen towards her and gently held her by the shoulders. Then he turned her slowly and lowered his forehead to rest it against hers. 'I'm sorry, Maddy. This is why I say I'm selfish. I want you on my terms—not yours. I don't have time for settling down in nests. I'm always on the move, taking risks, sleeping in huts in war-torn villages. It's not a world I can share on a day-to-day basis.'

'We've been through this before, Rick.' Maddy slipped out of his grasp and crossed to where her coffee cup still stood on the kitchen bench. She took a sip, but the coffee had cooled, so she tipped it down the sink. She felt numb—as if a doctor had just confirmed her worst fears and now her hold on life was threatened. Now, all she could do was accept the facts and try to adjust to this new reality. 'It sounds like your mother has sussed us out as well,' she said.

'She warned me against trifling with your affections,' he concurred. 'She reminded me to think about what I want from life.'

Maddy stared at the floorboards and when she spoke she willed her voice to stay calm. 'She's right. I guess we just have to face up to the truth, Rick. We have two choices.' She took a deep breath. 'We can have a casual relationship—and—and I can handle that. Or I go home now and we don't see each other any more.'

It was surprising how easily she could say this, given the sense of desperation she felt. She looked up to find Rick's hard grey gaze fixed on her. It seemed he had nothing to say.

'I'll still come out and keep an eye on the property over the next couple of weeks,' she told him. 'Until you get back.'

His jaw stiffened, but he remained silent.

'You might like to ring Sam and see if he's interested...' The words caught in her throat. She'd started out bravely, but didn't know how much longer she could keep this up. 'So—so what do you think, Rick?'

He still didn't speak, but from the tension in his face, in his shoulders and in his clenched hands Maddy could sense that he was trying to control his emotions. She stood with her back to the sink, her hands pressed hard against her thighs.

'I think I'm a total idiot,' Rick said at last, 'but I'm going to let you go, Maddy.'

Her legs almost gave way. As she clutched at the sink for support, she felt the blood drain from her face.

'I don't want to lose you, but I'm so damned scared that I'll make you promises I can't keep.'

'You'd always be pining to take off somewhere more exciting,' Maddy supplied.

'It's more than likely,' Rick sighed. He moved to walk towards her, to take her in his arms, but Maddy backed away.

'I'd rather you didn't touch me,' she whispered.

His hands slapped to his sides and he shook his head. In his eyes, Maddy saw a terrible torment, but she couldn't help him.

He couldn't help her.

'Goodbye, Rick.' She turned and walked slowly out of the room.

'You're a miracle worker, Maddy.' Two weeks later, Sam stood on the steps of Torrington and held his arms wide in welcome. 'I would never have believed a bloke could get this lucky.'

Maddy was embraced in a bear hug. 'You're happy to be here, I take it?'

'Over the moon. Come and have a cuppa. Tea's already made.' Sam led her through to the kitchen.

At the sight of the scrubbed pine table, the old-fashioned wood stove and the jaunty yellow curtains of Torrington's kitchen, Maddy felt her body stiffen. Tension seized every part of her—legs, backbone, shoulders, jaw—so that she had to force herself to move across the floor and to take the seat Sam offered.

Two weeks ago she'd walked out of here feeling as if she'd been sentenced to solitary confinement for the term of her natural life. Today she didn't feel much better. She hadn't been able to eat or sleep properly.

'I can't thank you enough for sweet-talking Rick into inviting me to be caretaker.'

'There wasn't much sweet talk,' Maddy mumbled as she accepted a cup of tea.

'Oh?' Sam's head cocked to one side and he frowned at her.

Her response had been automatic and immediately she regretted it. She fluttered her hand in a tiny gesture of dismissal and then fiddled with the cup's handle. 'Rick and I—we've never been more than friends.'

While his eyes remained fixed on hers, Sam placed his cup carefully on its saucer. 'And you're happy with that?'

She shrugged. 'Of course.'

'That boy's a fool,' sighed Sam, shaking his head sadly.

It was more than Maddy could bear. She pushed the chair back from the table. 'Look, I came here to take a look at the property. I'm worried that the firebreaks are all overgrown. It's practically summer and, at this time of the year, there's always a danger of bushfires.'

'Too right. Can't be too careful,' agreed Sam, his expression suddenly businesslike. 'Bushfires can spring up out of nowhere. I covered the Ash Wednesday fires in Victoria and South Australia and I'll never forget them. It all happened so quickly. Seventy-two people dead, two thousand homes lost. It was probably the worst disaster I've filmed anywhere and I've seen a few.'

'I'll take a look around today and then I'll probably be back with my brother to clear the firebreaks with the tractor.'

Sam's jaw dropped. 'You can do that kind of thing?'

'Sure, Sam. Don't look like that. I grew up on a farm.' She held out her hand. 'Do you have the keys to the truck?'

The old-fashioned phone attached to the kitchen wall pealed before Sam could respond.

'Excuse me,' he said, hopping up to answer it. He lifted the receiver. 'Oh, Rick? Good to hear from you. You still in Hong Kong?' His eyes darted quickly to Maddy.

A huge, painful lump formed in her throat as she sat, frozen to the chair. Even though she desperately wanted to get up and run, a dreadful curiosity held her. As Sam continued to speak, she listened with awful fascination to his end of the conversation.

'Sure, I've settled in really well, mate.' Sam was nodding as he spoke. 'This farm of your mum's is terrific. I'm as cosy as a possum in a hollow log.'

There was more silence as he listened to the voice coming down the line. 'Bushfires? That's the bad news,' Sam said with a sigh. 'The whole east coast is like a tinder box. They're already having really bad fires down in Victoria. Three people killed. It's terrible. Maddy's pretty worried about this place... Maddy? Of course I've seen her. She's here now. You want to talk to her?'

'*No!*' cried Maddy. How could Sam do this to her? But it appeared from Sam's restraining hand gestures that Rick was no keener to engage in conversation than she was.

Sam continued to yell his news into the phone. 'She's planning to work on this property with her younger brother. They're going to hitch a slasher onto the tractor and clear all the firebreaks. None too soon either. The mercury's rising through the roof this summer. And no sign of a wet season yet. I'd work on the breaks myself, but I don't think I'm quite up to that kind of caper just yet.'

Once more there was silence while Sam listened to Rick. Maddy sipped her tea and nervously crumbled the biscuit Sam had given her.

'Yeah.' Sam was nodding his head in agreement. 'That woman's a class act, all right.' He shot a little self-conscious smile her way as he continued talking. 'But tell me, mate, what's going on between you two? I sense trouble in the waters.'

'*Sam, stay out of it!*' she cried angrily.

He must have had a similar reaction from Rick. The next minute he was shaking his head and letting out a long, slow whistle as he stared at Maddy in dismay. 'For Pete's sake, Rick, you need your head read. You're turning this sweet little thing down? You'll never meet another girl like Maddy in this lifetime.'

The response on the other end of the line must have been explosive. The conversation ended with a distinctly impatient grumble from Sam.

As soon as Sam replaced the phone, Maddy jumped to her feet.

'Before I get a lecture from you, let my ear recover from the one I've just had,' he pleaded, patting his ear with a rueful smile.

Maddy was quite willing to drop the whole subject of Rick Lawson. 'If you could give me the key to the truck, I'll have a quick look round and then I need to head back to town,' she said.

Sam limped across the room to select a key from the assortment hanging near the back door. He shot Maddy a quizzical look. 'Don't go breaking your heart just yet, Maddy. Our young Rick just can't see the wood from the trees.'

She rolled her eyes to the ceiling. It helped to hold back the sudden threat of tears. 'What are you implying, Sam?'

Sam looked at the key in his hand and tossed it. 'I'm not just implying something, I *know* something.'

'Which is?'

'My famous mate's not nearly as smart as he thinks he is. He's usually so calm and collected, no matter what crisis he's facing. But right now he's more stirred up than a nest of bulldog ants. It's plain as day he's in love with you.'

'Oh, give up, Sam,' Maddy shouted as she stomped towards the door.

CHAPTER EIGHT

BUSHFIRES were breaking out all over the country. The reports of spreading fires were in every newspaper and on every television bulletin.

Chrissie was able to work extra hours for Maddy so she could get away from the shop to clear the breaks on Torrington. But time was running out. Big fires had already started in the Brisbane hinterland.

What particularly worried Maddy was the fact that there hadn't been any bad bushfires through the region for some time, so there was plenty of litter—dead leaves, dry twigs and fallen branches. It was the kind of fuel these fires gobbled up. And the persistent heatwave conditions around Brisbane for the past week made the situation even more serious. It was all they needed for a really bad burn.

Sitting on the steps of the Torrington farmhouse, she drank another of Sam's cups of tea. 'The local volunteer fire brigade is calling for help,' she told him. ''I think I should join up.'

'Oh, my God,' he groaned. 'Rick would never forgive me if I let you get involved with them.'

'Rick's got nothing to do with this,' she replied angrily.

'You know he's being brought back to cover the international angle of the bushfire story?'

'No, I didn't.' Maddy held the teacup tightly against her chest, so Sam couldn't see the way her hands began to shake at his news. 'I've been properly trained to work in rural fire brigades,' she added in an effort to reassure him. He looked so dreadfully worried. 'They're very strict about that. But apparently they need all the help they can get. I'll only be involved in helping to fight grass fires in this district.'

Sam's mouth drooped and his shoulders sagged as he offered her an apologetic smile. 'I can tell by that determined glint in your eye that it's no use trying to stop you.'

'No, Sam, you can't. And I'm off to help them as soon as I finish this tea.'

By late afternoon, Maddy was wondering how wise she'd been to race off fighting fires. She'd never felt more exhausted in her life. Every part of her body ached, her eyes were stinging from coping with smoke and flying grit and her mouth was dry and dusty.

With a grateful sigh, she pulled off her helmet and wriggled her shoulders free from the straps of her water knapsack with its spray gun attachment. Then she lowered herself onto the ash-strewn dirt, and took long sips from her water bottle. Every pore on her body screamed for a long, soothing relax in a sudsy bath.

But it was a short-lived reprieve. Their group leader approached her and the other weary fighters. 'There's a really big blaze started up in the forest between Jefferies Road and the highway,' he told them. 'They want us up there straight away. All available tankers in this district are needed.' He tried to crack an encouraging smile.

Maddy suppressed a groan. She doubted she had the strength to pull herself to her feet. It wasn't just the firefighting taking its toll; she'd been pushing herself to the limit all week—trying to keep her business running as well as helping to clear the breaks on Torrington.

Then there was the Rick Lawson factor.

She'd done her best to concentrate on practical problems and to push memories of Rick's final, chilling rejection out of her mind. But it was a fairly useless exercise. Trying to forget Rick took up every drop of her emotional and mental reserves. A surge of despair swept over her. Perhaps it wouldn't matter if something terrible happened to her today. She hadn't much to live for anyhow.

But once they reached the new location she had little time for reflection. All hell broke loose within twenty minutes of their arrival.

Maddy had gone back to the fire truck to refill her water knapsack, when the cries of alarm broke out behind her. She turned to see a huge wall of sickening flames only two hundred metres away and racing at breakneck speed towards them. A towering blood-red wave roared through the bush, eating up everything in its path. For several seconds she was so gripped by crippling panic that she couldn't move, couldn't think, couldn't remember any of her training.

The men were running towards her, their shapes black silhouettes against the hideous backdrop of glowing fire. As the terrifying hiss and boom of the flames crescendoed, Maddy swallowed, trying to ease the searing dryness in her parched throat. What should she do?

And then suddenly her mind cleared. She didn't stop to reconsider, but ran to the truck. She had to pick up the men and drive them to a clearing. Her feet took off before her mind had finished planning the details. The radiant heat was horrific. Maddy wrenched the door open and a scream of pain tore from her lips as her hands met the scalding metal. But there wasn't time to worry about any injury. She flicked the key in the ignition switch and felt a surge of gratitude as the motor immediately kicked to life.

Edging the truck forward, she reached the racing, gasping men. It seemed to take for ever while they clambered into the truck. The smoke reached them first, ahead of the flames, and Maddy could feel her chest heaving.

There was yelling all around her. Maddy pressed her foot to the accelerator once more and steered blindly into the smoke pall. She had no idea now if she was heading in the direction of the clearing; all she knew was that she had to try to keep ahead of that roaring, terrible monster bearing down on them.

'You can pull up now, Maddy,' she heard someone yell from behind. 'We'll turn the truck's water jets on and sit it out. Good luck, everyone.'

Through the dreadful black, suffocating smoke and the roar of the flames all around them, Maddy thought she heard another sound. The chug-chug-chug of a helicopter. She peered through the windscreen, trying to catch a glimpse of a black shape hovering above them.

'Bloody media,' someone muttered. 'They'd be a lot more help if they got down here.'

It was almost impossible to breathe. The searing skin on Maddy's hands was unbearable and she was feeling dizzy. Her last thought before the roaring red conflagration engulfed them and she blacked out completely was to wonder if Rick was up there in the helicopter.

'Maddy! Maddy, can you hear me?'

Who was calling her? Maddy could hear her name but the voice seemed to come from miles away. She tried to answer, but couldn't make any sound. Her throat hurt and her head ached. Everything ached. What was the matter with her?

'Maddy, sweetheart, it's me. Rick.'

Rick? She forced her eyes to open, but everything was blurry, so she allowed them to drift shut again.

'Thank God, she's alive,' she heard Rick say.

Where was Rick? Perhaps if she tried to sit up? Piercing agony shot through her hands and she heard someone moaning. *She* was moaning.

'Watch her hands. They're badly burnt.' That was a different voice.

And suddenly, in a rush, Maddy remembered the fire…and the terror…dashing to the truck…

'Let's get her out of here quickly.' She could hear Rick again. 'What can we cover her hands with?'

Someone was wrapping her hands very gently, lifting her tenderly. It was a man who held her—it had to be Rick. Somehow she was quite certain of that. She could sense the strength in his arms and chest as he carried her carefully, so as not to bump her hands. He was bending his face to hers and his warm lips brushed her cheek. 'You're going to be fine, Maddy,' he whispered. 'Don't worry. We'll have you out of here in a jiffy.'

Slowly she opened her eyes again. Yes, there was Rick's lovely, familiar profile. She tried to speak. Her voice croaked, 'How did you get here?' and then she coughed.

'Rest your throat,' he urged. 'Just relax. I'll fill you in on all the details later. Let's get you up into the chopper first.' Then she heard him call to someone else. 'We'll take her to the nearest hospital.'

As he carried her, fresh air fanned her face and greedily she sucked in the cooling draught. That felt better.

More hands were lifting her. If only her *own* hands weren't so painful.

Around her, voices circled.

'I'd say she's mainly suffering from heat exhaustion and the burns to her hands,' she heard her group leader explain. 'She saved our lives, you know.'

'We thought we were done for.'

'What happened?'

'We were all busy fighting the fire, but Maddy was closest to the tanker. When the fireball came bursting towards us, she ran to the truck and drove it over to the rest of us just in time. It was quick thinking on her part.'

'And damn plucky.'

'What about her hands? How did that happen?' she heard Rick ask.

'They were burnt when she first opened the driver's door. But she didn't hesitate.'

As she felt herself lowered to the helicopter seat, Maddy looked up at Rick again. His eyes were bright and glittering. 'That's my girl,' he murmured tenderly, tucking a stray strand of hair away from her eyes. 'Always lending a helping hand.'

Then she heard the helicopter's motor roar to life and felt the craft sway as it lifted off the ground. Maddy closed her eyes again. It was all too hard to try to take in the details of the cabin's interior and focus on strange faces. And it was impossible to understand the concern and emotion she read in Rick's eyes.

She was puzzled and needed to think. Why was Rick here in the middle of a bushfire and being so nice to her? At that moment, her mind felt as if it was caught in one of her brother's computer games, running down endless paths and coming to dead ends. Every so often, like a horrific monster from the game, a memory would jump out and confuse her more than ever. The most consistent memory was of the last time she'd seen Rick. She was certain he'd been heading for Hong Kong and telling her he didn't want to see her anymore.

Yes, that *was* right. She could never get that part wrong. It was all over between her and Rick. She could never forget that awful night—driving away from Torrington, with tears streaming so madly down her face that she'd wished she had windscreen wipers for her eyes.

It was all too difficult to think about…easier to just sleep…

Maddy only had sketchy memories of the trip to the hospital and what followed. There was a stretcher, uniformed attendants, Rick hovering nearby, looking white-faced…soothing ointment, painkillers, endless bandaging of her hands…

Eventually she was tucked between crisp white sheets with her heavily bandaged hands resting on the bedcovers.

'You need to rest,' a nurse assured her. 'You've been suffering from heat exposure and we're keeping you here for a few days because you can't look after yourself very well with both hands bandaged.'

Maddy nodded. She would be happy to rest for a while.

'That is, unless you would really like to leave,' the nurse added cautiously. 'There's a man outside who is quite adamant that he can look after you.'

'A man?' Maddy asked wondering if it could possibly be Rick.

'A Mr Lawson. He claims to be a close friend.'

For a moment Maddy almost weakened. She longed to see Rick again. If he wanted to look after her, she could think of nothing better. But she had to be sensible. The time for useless dreaming was over. He had told her they had no future and it would be the worst form of torment to pretend anything had changed just because she'd had a little accident. 'He's mistaken,' she said as calmly as she could. 'Mr Lawson is only an acquaintance. I don't know him very well at all. I'd prefer to stay here.'

'That's perfectly all right, dear. Don't worry. I never let these masterful types bully me.' She re-tucked a corner of Maddy's perfectly tucked sheet. 'We'll contact your family of course.'

By the next morning Maddy was feeling pretty much her normal self.

'You're quite a celebrity,' a pretty nurse with short red hair told her as she breezed into her room. 'Look at you—surrounded by all these beautiful flower arrangements and the florists have hardly opened their doors. And now your photo's in the paper as well.'

'She's a hero, that's why,' came a deep voice from behind the nurse. Maddy looked up to see the doorway filled with a mass of roses—white, red, yellow, pink. There had to be at least two dozen of each colour. 'Morning, Maddy,' beamed Rick, poking his head around the mountain of blooms.

'My goodness.' Maddy gulped. Rick was looking at her so anxiously, she felt warm and shivery inside.

'That's a bunch and a half,' agreed the nurse. Then she eyed Rick shrewdly before taking Maddy's wrist to check her pulse. 'I hope you're not allergic to flowers.'

'Oh, no chance of that,' Maddy laughed.

'But something's making your pulse race,' the nurse muttered moments later as she leant to straighten Maddy's pillow. She glanced at Rick again and then quickly back at Maddy. 'This visitor doesn't upset you?' she whispered.

'N-no.' Maddy's response was automatic. Now wasn't the time to admit to being constantly upset by Rick Lawson.

Rick suffered another careful scrutiny as the girl left the room and in response he pulled a face at her retreating back and shut the door behind her.

Maddy shook her head at the enormous bouquet. 'Good heavens, Rick, these are all for me? I thought I was used to flowers, but this bunch is amazing.'

'And bought from the very best florist in town,' he said, with a wink.

'You must have bought every rose in the shop. So, how's Chrissie managing?'

Rick smiled and shrugged simultaneously. 'She's been overrun with orders this morning.' He looked around the room. 'And I can see why.'

'Our sales figures for this week will certainly look good,' Maddy agreed. 'I think all of these flowers have come from Floral Fantasies. There's a lovely arrangement from Sam—and he added a note to say that Torrington is fine.'

Rick nodded. 'I checked with him last night. Thanks so much for pushing those breaks through, Maddy. I don't know how on earth you got it all done.'

'Andy helped,' she replied dismissively. 'My parents have sent lovely flowers, too, and there's even an arrangement from the rural fire brigade... By the way, how are the rest of the fires?'

'Just about all burnt out. Yesterday saw the worst of it. A lot of forest area's been damaged, and some property, but no lives lost, thank goodness.' He placed the roses on a chair in the corner of the room and perched on the side of her bed, looking at her with a shy, uncertain smile. 'More importantly,' he said, 'how are you?'

'Much better,' she replied brightly, although with him sitting so close she felt a little giddy again. 'Right as rain really. My hands are so beautifully bandaged, I can't feel a thing.'

He nodded silently and, to Maddy's surprise, he blinked his eyes...as if...something in his eye was bothering him.

'How are *you*, Rick?'

'Oh! Never better.' He saw the newspaper on her bedside table. 'Do you want me to read what they had to say about you in the local rag?'

At her nod, Rick opened the newspaper and began to read her the story. Maddy felt her cheeks blaze to hear herself described in such heroic terms. He finished rather abruptly.

'Doesn't it have anything there about the way you rescued me?'

Rick quickly refolded the paper. 'Ah—one or two lines. But you know how the press like to beat these things up.'

'And that's an opinion straight from the horse's mouth,' Maddy reminded him.

His eyes darted back to the pile of roses. 'I—er—know that flowers don't really do the trick for you, Maddy—because you work with them all the time. I'm—um—working on something better, but it still needs a bit of polishing.'

'Polishing? Rick, what on earth do you mean?'

He stood up and his long brown fingers twisted a knob on the railing at the end of her bed. 'You'll see,' came his eventual, unhelpful response. 'Actually, I'd better get going. Still got work to do, I'm afraid.'

Surprised at this new, fumbling and nervous Rick, Maddy hardly knew how to respond. He was probably realising that now she was out of danger they had reverted to their uneasy and futile relationship. A relationship that was completely finished. 'Of course you must get back to work. Thanks for the flowers. And—thanks so much for yesterday.'

His shoulders rose in a brief shrug and a smile flickered momentarily as he took two steps towards her, then halted. 'I'll catch you later,' he said softly, before turning and hurrying out of the room.

Talk about seesawing emotions, Maddy thought as she lay in the starched white bed, pondering Rick's behaviour and her reactions to it. Yesterday she'd been thrilled to see him again and to know it was his quick action that had swept her so speedily to safety. Today she was swamped with memories of their old arguments.

It didn't matter how sweet he was to her, or how badly she needed him—the bottom line was that they had no future. Travelling all round the world, trying to keep up with Rick, would be a lifestyle fraught with problems. Much and all as she loved him, Maddy was too practical to think that it would work.

She should be grateful that his visit had been so fleeting.

When the nurse returned to change her dressings and bandages, she frowned at Maddy. 'You look a bit low.'

'I'm still a little tired, that's all. It's been a big week.'

'Rick Lawson wasn't making a nuisance of himself this morning, was he?'

Why did the mention of his name make her cheeks flush? It was so embarrassing. 'No—no, not at all.'

'I just don't trust journalists,' the nurse added as she examined Maddy's hand. 'This is looking good. I don't think there will be any scarring in the long run.' She looked up from her work. 'We've had the press making a nuisance of themselves in here too many times. He won't be turning up here with television cameras and miles of cables, disrupting the whole ward, will he?'

'No,' Maddy reassured her. 'He probably won't be back at all. But he certainly won't be wanting to film me.'

'I must say, he's jolly nice-looking,' the girl conceded as she carefully rebandaged Maddy's hand. 'He has the cutest smile. And he does put together a very interesting program. I know whenever one of his documentaries is on television the doctors are always discussing it the next day in the canteen.'

'Yes, he's very good at his job,' Maddy agreed, and tried very hard not to sound glum.

Her mother visited her shortly after that. She brought three pretty new nightgowns and helped Maddy to manage her lunch and they had a lovely hour catching up on all the news about the farm, family and friends.

'You'll have to come home to us as soon as you leave here. It would be lovely to have you home for your father's birthday, but, more importantly, I want to make sure you don't start trying to do too much too soon.'

'That probably would be sensible, Mum. And I'd love to see Dad. But I must check how Chrissie is coping without me.'

'Don't get too worried about that, darling. I'm going straight to the shop from here.'

Maddy was grateful for her mother's concern, and she tried to squash down the foolish thought that she might not want her family too close at hand if Rick was still around...

As Anita Delancy bent to kiss her daughter goodbye, another nurse burst into the room—a bubbly girl with wispy blonde hair. 'A special delivery for Madeline,' she announced with a wide grin. She was holding something behind her back.

'Let me take it,' offered Maddy's mother.

The girl hesitated for a moment then brought forward a bright pink envelope. She held it up for Maddy to see her name scrawled inside a large heart. 'It's a bit early for Valentine's Day,' she giggled.

Maddy could feel herself blushing again, especially when she saw the way her mother's eyes widened. 'Just leave it on my bedside table, thanks,' she told the nurse.

'Wouldn't you like me to open it for you?' asked her mother as soon as the nurse left.

Good grief, no! Maddy had recognised Rick's handwriting. It would have been different if Rick loved her. Then she would have been happy to tell her mother all about him. But now she shook her head frantically. 'No, Mum. It's all right, thanks. It's—it's probably some crank who read the story in the paper. I—I'd like to rest now. I'll take a look at it later.'

'If you're sure, dear.' Anita Delancy was having difficulty hiding her curiosity. Her eyes, dark like Maddy's, kept darting to the pink envelope. 'Well, I'm sure you need your rest,' she murmured, not sounding sure at all. When Maddy made no response, she picked up her handbag and straightened her shoulders. 'I'm off to Floral Fantasies, then, to see what I can do to help there.'

'That would be great, Mum. It was lovely to see you. But don't worry about me, please. I'm fine.'

Her mother had barely left the room before Maddy

reached for the envelope, her heart racketing around crazily. What on earth was Rick up to?

Bringing her two bandaged hands together like awkward, fluffy tongs, she carefully lifted the envelope, but it was so difficult to feel the thin paper through the heavy bandaging. Just when she thought she held it safely, it slipped from her grasp, fluttering to the floor.

Maddy swore. She was feeling desperate, so, with her knees, she pushed the bedclothes aside and swung her legs out of the bed. But it was going to be harder than ever to pick up Rick's mail now.

'Were you wanting to go to the bathroom?'

Maddy swung round to see the blonde nurse's cheery face poking around the door. 'Er, no,' she said, 'I—'

'Oh!' cried the girl, seeing the paper on the floor. 'Here, let me get it for you. You hop back into bed.' As she stooped to pick up the envelope, she beamed at Maddy. 'I *love* romantic men. But there aren't enough to go around. Would you like me to open this for you? I promise I won't read a word.'

Acknowledging defeat, Maddy nodded as she clambered back onto the bed. There was no way she could manage this alone.

A single page of pink writing paper emerged.

'Here you are. Bend your knees and I'll prop this against your lap for you. How's that?'

Maddy weakly smiled her thanks, but even before the nurse discreetly left the room she was reading.

Before you,
I saw the same sea, sky and hills
and didn't know
you lived and breathed on this
sweet planet.

> But now,
> having met you,
> loved you,
> I cannot walk this Earth
> knowing you
> are where I am not.

She read it five times before her eyes blurred with tears and it became impossible to see the words. *Oh, Rick!* Maddy sank back onto the pillow. She felt sick. Was Rick really trying to say that he loved her? She squeezed her eyes shut to hold back the tears.

Mopping at her wet cheeks with her bandaged hand, Maddy struggled to understand. Was Rick feeling sorry for her? Perhaps that was it. He was upset by the accident and her helplessness and somehow he felt responsible. Rick had always had a very highly developed conscience.

He couldn't possibly mean what this poem seemed to be saying.

If he had done something like this when we first met, she thought wistfully, *I would have been swept off my feet. But not now. How could he mess me around like this now? He knows our future is hopeless. He was the one who made that final decision. He knows he has no real place for me in his life. By the time I get out of hospital he'll probably be gone again.*

She ground her teeth in frustration. They'd discussed it so many times already and it always came back to the same answer. The best they could ever hope for would be a long affair, but they both knew that would break her heart.

CHAPTER NINE

MADDY wasn't particularly surprised when Rick hurried into her room that evening, looking illegally handsome in a business suit. She had, by then, resurrected a measure of composure. But her heart still flipped at the sight of him.

His greeting was unexpected. 'You haven't eaten, have you?'

'No, I haven't,' she replied, eyeing him cautiously. 'Actually I'm surprised I haven't had dinner yet. Usually hospital meals come ridiculously early.'

'That's a relief. They got my message, then.'

'Oh? *They* might have,' she replied with deliberate cool, 'but I didn't. What's going on, Rick?'

'I'll show you.' His smile rippled over her, coating her with unexpected warmth. 'Let me help you up.'

Maddy was grateful that she'd bathed and changed into one of the demure nightgowns her mother had brought her. Sensibly high-necked, with short sleeves, it still looked pretty, with its deep trims of lacy cream ruffles.

'How are you on your feet?' he asked.

'Absolutely fine. The only reason they're keeping me here is because I'm so useless without my hands.'

'Well, you won't need them tonight,' he grinned. 'This way.'

Rick rested his hand on her back and steered her down the corridor. Maddy could feel the heat of his touch through the thin fabric of her nightgown and she willed her body not to react. But it seemed she was very weak-willed.

They reached two curtained French doors. With a flourish, he opened them to reveal a small balcony looking down into the main hospital quadrangle below. Right in the middle of the balcony was a table set for two with gleaming silver, flowers, candlesticks, and an ice bucket sporting a bottle of champagne.

'For us?' Maddy's exclamation sounded more like a strangled gasp.

'Of course.' Rick grinned broadly.

'But, Rick, for heaven's sake. This is a hospital. You can't just set up a restaurant wherever you feel like it.'

'Oh, but you can if you speak to the right people.'

'What—what kind of people?'

'Your doctor for starters. Apparently he's a fan of mine. And he agreed this would do you the world of good.'

'I'm allowed to drink champagne?'

'A glass or two are just what the doctor ordered.'

The dreadful tears that had been plaguing her all afternoon threatened again. There had been too many surprises in one day. Maddy wondered whether she was strong enough for more. She began to wish she hadn't made such an obvious and dramatic recovery. Physically she might seem well, but she knew that if her emotional state were assessed she would be on the critical list.

She offered a feeble protest. 'But—but I can't manage cutlery…'

Rick's smile was dangerously sexy. 'That won't be a problem, Maddy.' He pulled out her chair and, as she sat down, he spoke softly in her ear. 'I'm looking forward to feeding you dainty morsels with my own hands.'

Her stomach started to flutter. 'Oh? So I'm to be a captive diner?'

'It's one of my fantasies.'

That silenced her.

Rick took his seat and removed the cork from the champagne bottle. As the pale wine bubbled into thin crystal flutes, Maddy felt compelled to bring up the subject of the special-delivery mail. She couldn't just pretend it had never arrived.

'I didn't know you were a poet, Rick.'

He had the grace to look embarrassed. 'I'm not really, am I?'

She smiled, warmed by the shaft of uncertainty that crossed his face. It made him look much younger and more vulnerable. 'I wouldn't expect you to be installed as Poet Laureate just yet,' she said gently, hoping to make light of the matter.

'Ah.' He smiled slowly. 'But you know what they say. It's the thought that counts.'

Maddy gnawed at her lower lip. The *thoughts* expressed in his poem were the problem. They were turning her inside out. 'Yes,' she said softly. 'The thoughts were...were charming.'

His eyes held hers as he lifted her glass to her lips. 'Here's to your health, Maddy.'

The champagne was delicious—dry and beautifully chilled. Rick drank from his own glass. 'And here's to us.' There was a wistful strain in his voice.

'What's for dinner?' she asked brightly, wondering just how she'd hold herself together if the evening became too deep and meaningful. She was determined to keep their conversation away from subjects that could only lead them down one-way streets to finally crash straight into dead ends.

Rick lifted the silver lid from a large platter. Bite-sized pieces of seafood and crisp stir-fried vegetables rested on a bed of fluffy rice. Maddy sniffed appreciatively as the aroma of delicate Asian spices wafted from the platter.

Spearing a succulent calamari ring, Rick held it up to her mouth. She took it between her teeth and chewed hungrily. 'Mmm, yum,' she murmured. 'This is delicious, Rick.'

The food *was* delicious, but Maddy was very afraid that the method of eating would wreck her digestion. Rick's eyes hadn't left her lips and, with her hands out of action, she couldn't even dab at them with her linen napkin. She licked her lower lip and the movement of her tongue seemed to hold his complete attention.

'Don't forget you must eat, too,' she said, a little too quickly, and caught the amusement in his eyes as he helped himself to some fish and a swig of champagne.

Then he offered her more food and drink. The doctor was probably right. This delicious seafood, the quiet balcony and Rick's slow lazy smile were a wonderful tonic after the boring hospital room. She felt the fizzing champagne bubbles shooting through her, helping her to relax.

'Close your eyes, Maddy,' Rick murmured. 'See if you can guess what kind of seafood this is.'

Maddy hesitated, then obeyed. A sweet round sea scallop, coated with a delightfully mild chili and ginger sauce, slipped into her mouth. She chewed with genuine enjoyment. 'That's a scallop,' she laughed. 'I love them. Can I have another one, please?' It was even easier to relax with her eyes closed. She didn't have to feel confused by the clear message of desire gleaming in Rick's eyes.

'Keep your eyes closed, Maddy,' Rick murmured. 'Here comes a prawn.'

'I feel like a baby bird in its nest,' she laughed.

She heard Rick's chuckle. 'I can assure you, I don't feel remotely like a mother bird.' His voice was low and husky.

Maddy munched happily. She was beginning to enjoy herself. With her eyes closed and Rick's warm voice coaxing her, she could almost pretend they had no problems and that their love was real.

At some point—she wasn't quite sure when—Rick must have put his fork aside and begun to feed her with his fingers. And, when his warm fingers lingered on her lips, a throb of unsettling excitement stirred to life low within her. She couldn't resist the urge to lick the sauce from them. The taste of his skin and the feel of his fingers in her mouth proved even more intoxicating than the wine.

She heard the sharp intake of his breath and her heart picked up pace.

'I'm sure it must be very sinful to eat this way,' she whispered.

'It's certainly very sensual...very...'

'Very oral?' Maddy supplied, and was immediately very grateful that her eyes were still closed, so she couldn't see Rick's reaction.

But she felt it.

Rick moved to her side in a moment. 'Maddy,' he whispered. And she felt his hands frame her face and his lips join hers. When his mouth caressed her, it was as if she'd never been kissed before. In mere seconds, she was aroused to a dizzying fever pitch. Surely the earth was moving, fireworks were exploding and angelic choruses were bursting into glorious song? Rick tasted so right!

Maddy felt so very, very right.

'My goodness,' Rick breathed against her cheek. 'I've never believed in magic. But...when we kiss...' Kneeling beside her, he rested his forehead against hers and drew in a deep sigh. 'How do you do it, Maddy? One little touch of your magic lips and you change me into...'

'A handsome prince?' Deliriously happy, she rubbed her nose against his cheek.

He chuckled softly and reached into his pocket. Moving her plate to one side, he placed a small parcel wrapped in pink tissue paper on the table in front of her. 'You change me into a man who wants to try to be excessively romantic,' he said.

Still trembling from the impact of his kiss, Maddy stared in disbelief as Rick tore away the paper to expose a small box. It was made of exquisite gold filigree and when Rick lifted the lid he revealed deep green lining and a delicate figurine turning in time to a wistful, tinkling tune.

'What a darling music box,' Maddy cried, delighted. She tilted her head as she listened to the tune. 'That music. I can't quite place it, but it seems vaguely familiar.'

'I'm not sure what it's called,' admitted Rick. 'But I heard it playing in a shop in Hong Kong and I didn't know enough Cantonese to find out its name, but I just had to buy it. It's the music we danced to at the party. It's our tune, Maddy.'

'Goodness, Rick,' Maddy whispered. 'Fancy remembering. That really *is* an excessively romantic gesture.'

He took his place sitting opposite her again and

smiled. 'I'm glad you think so. That's what I'm working on.'

Maddy felt completely overwhelmed. Her emotions were about to take flight, like a cluster of bright balloons sailing high on a sunny sky.

Caution!

In much the same manner as a traffic sign on the very edge of the highway, the warning flashed into Maddy's consciousness just in time. How could she sit here and be taken in by Rick's charm when she knew just how miserably she ended up whenever she allowed him to trifle with her affections?

'But I don't understand, Rick. Why are you doing this? What's it all about?'

Rick frowned as if he wasn't sure of himself. 'You should know, Maddy.'

Maddy felt her shoulders sag. He was going to make this difficult. 'I should?' she asked, her voice drooping with her dismay. She was totally puzzled now.

'You told me exactly what you wanted and I've done my damnedest to give it to you.'

'*I* told you I wanted all this?' Maddy cried in bewilderment, throwing her bandaged hands in the air and wincing slightly.

'Ages ago you outlined for me your idea of the perfect romantic male. Don't you remember?'

'Rick,' she said very slowly and carefully, as if she were talking to a very slow-witted child, 'I don't know what *you're* on about, but I'm talking about your strange behaviour today. First you bring me the biggest bunch of flowers in the Southern Hemisphere. Then you send me love—well—poetry. And tonight you wine me and dine me and now this lovely music box.'

'And it doesn't make any sense to you?' he asked softly, his eyes revealing a confusion of his own.

'Not one ounce!' cried Maddy. 'I mean, anyone would think...' She stopped and her jaw dropped. She stared at Rick as if he'd just explained, in perfectly clear and simple terms, Einstein's theory of relativity. 'Did you say *my* idea of the *perfect romantic male*?'

'Uh-huh.'

She slumped in her chair, suddenly quite exhausted.

Rick rushed back to her side. 'Let me carry you back to your room, Maddy. It's all been too much for you. I should have been more considerate. Hell, I was too busy worrying about *my* feelings.'

Maddy shook her head. 'Hold on, Rick. I'm all right.' She pulled a wry face. 'I've just figured out what you're up to.'

'You can't have forgotten the live-in-lover project?'

'And my definition of a truly romantic man.' Maddy held her bandaged hands up to her face and groaned. 'I said all that, didn't I?'

'Your list was quite specific, as I remember. You mentioned the poetry, the music, the dinner on the candlelit balcony.'

'But, Rick, I'm still confused. Surely that's all behind us? We don't have to go on pretending to be lovers now.'

Maddy saw Rick's expression stiffen. '*Maddy*, I'm not pretending.'

'Not pretending?' she repeated after a shocked moment.

'I stopped pretending long ago. I don't really think I've ever been pretending. It's just taken me a hell of a while to realise how I feel about you.'

Maddy closed her eyes to avoid the raw emotion in

Rick's face. How had this happened? This whole evening had been a wonderful but terrible trap. Like the most beautiful silken spider's web, Rick had spun an evening of magic and enchantment that had almost ensnared her.

But it was a trap she'd fallen into one too many times. It didn't matter how sweet and loving Rick was tonight; tomorrow he would be gone. And then there would be all the other tomorrows.

Sitting very straight in her chair, with her shoulders back and chin held high, she blinked away a tear. 'You say you didn't realise how you feel about me? So how do you feel, Rick?'

'Why, I love you of course. That's why I've tried to make this evening as romantic as possible.'

'Romance,' Maddy repeated dully, and her eyes searched the night sky.

'Isn't that what you wanted? You said your perfect live-in lover should be romantic.'

Maddy felt sick, confused, on the verge of a dreadful, teary breakdown. 'Oh, Rick. Are you sure all this is about romance?'

He sighed and ran a desperate finger around the inside of his collar. 'I admit I'm not overly imaginative,' he said. 'I'm more used to dealing with fact than fancy. Perhaps I should have had messages blown up in lights or something. And I know my poetry was a bit lacking in literary flair.' He tried to crack a grin, but it looked very forced. 'But at least I saved you from having to listen to my singing. I could understand that putting you off.'

He was rewarded by a tiny smile. Maddy leant towards him, her face earnest; her voice, when she spoke, was very shaky but very determined. 'Rick, I've done lots of dreaming about you, but, after Byron and...and our discussion out at Torrington, I've had too many reality checks this year to go on dreaming any longer. *I'm talking facts now.* And the fact is *nothing* has changed. Nothing is any different now than it was two weeks ago, when you told me we had no future. Except that now I've been injured in a fire.'

She saw Rick's face stiffen.

'I don't know,' Maddy rushed on. 'Maybe this is a guilt thing—maybe you feel sorry for me. Or maybe it's simply that you've played Prince Valiant one too many times and got carried away with the idea.'

'I wanted to give you a wonderful romantic experience, Maddy. I wasn't getting this night together for some poor little burns victim. It was for *you*.' He shoved back his chair and stood up, towering above her. Hands thrust in his pockets, he threw back his head and looked at the dark, star-studded sky as if searching for guidance in the heavens. When he looked at her again, his expression was fierce.

'I seem to be able to tell you how I feel more eloquently with my body than with words. Words have a way of being twisted, of being misunderstood.' His dark eyes speared her and she wished she could close her own eyes again.

Instead, she stood up, holding herself proudly erect. 'Your body is certainly very—persuasive,' she said in a tight, shaky little voice. 'And tonight was a wonderful idea, Rick. Don't get me wrong, I really do appreciate this lovely, lovely evening very much. But—' she blinked back the sudden rush of tears. 'But the bottom line is that you're still Rick Lawson, foreign correspondent extraordinaire! And by the time I get out of hospital you'll probably be in—in Israel or Antarctica or somewhere just as far-flung. Remember last time we had this discussion? You said you wanted love and romance on your terms.'

'But now I know that I love you.'

For a moment Maddy thought she might lose the battle with her tears. Her face began to crumple and her lip trembled. She forced herself to concentrate on the pattern in the lace edge of the tablecloth until the hot pricking behind her eyes lessened and she knew she was not going to make a fool of herself. She shook her head slowly, sadly. 'Goodnight, Rick.' Turning towards the door, she looked back at him over the frilly ruffle on one shoulder. His face was very pale. 'I'm going back to my ward now and I'd prefer it if you didn't come.'

CHAPTER TEN

Two days later, Sam ambled into Maddy's hospital room just as she arrived back from taking a walk in the grounds, and she was surprised at the rush of affection she felt at the sight of his friendly grin.

'It's great to see you,' she cried with genuine warmth.

'And it's always good to see you, Maddy.'

'You only just caught me. I'm being discharged this evening. Look, I can wiggle my fingers again.' She held out her hands.

Sam frowned and shook his head as he examined them. 'So, how are you feeling now?'

'Wonderful. It was so good to get rid of all that heavy bandaging. My left hand wasn't too badly burnt at all, so I just have to keep a dressing on my palm. The right hand will take a little longer, but I won't have to have skin grafts or anything messy like that.' Maddy paused for breath and smiled apologetically. 'So that's the medical report. Come and sit down, Sam, and tell me how the property went in the fires.'

'The property's hunky-dory,' Sam told her. 'Your firebreaks did the trick and a late thunderstorm put out any final threats.' Maddy watched as Sam's gaze wandered around the room. 'You know,' he said after a moment, 'it's funny, isn't it? Our roles have reversed. We met when you were visiting *me* in hospital.'

'Yes,' Maddy answered slowly, and a second later she was praying silently that Sam would not use this recollection as an excuse to bring Rick into the conversation.

She couldn't bear to go through a post-mortem of their disastrous relationship.

As expected, she hadn't heard from Rick after she'd sent him away.

'I guess it's too hot to do much planting just now,' she added quickly in a bid to keep the conversation safe.

Sam nodded in reply and he eyed her speculatively. Any moment now she just knew he would start talking about Rick. And she would have to find a way not to cry.

'So you're settling down for a long, hot summer on Torrington, Sam?'

'Sure am,' he grinned. 'This time last year we were in the middle of a war zone. I'm rather looking forward to a quiet time. I'd kind of like to be really ordinary this year—I'm going to watch all the soaps on the TV and have an occasional drink with the old fellow on the next property. It will be so good just pottering around the place and not having to dodge bullets.'

Maddy smiled and fiddled with the water jug on her bedside table as she willed her feeble mind not to dwell on the possibility of Rick in some war zone dodging bullets.

'And what about you, Maddy? Got any exciting plans when you get out of here?'

'I'm going home to be spoilt by my family.'

'Sounds...cosy.'

There was an awkward silence. The usually loquacious Sam seemed tense and lost for words. Perhaps keeping Rick out of their conversation was as difficult for him as it was for her. After all, Rick was the common link between them. Sam must have sensed her reluctance to discuss him.

He gently took her hands in his own. 'I certainly hope

you have a nice break and come back as good as new,' he said at last. 'I want to see that old twinkle back in your eye, Maddy.'

Oh, Sam, Maddy thought. *There's not much chance of that in the near future. I don't know if I will ever feel happy again.*

She stretched her features into the faint shadow of a smile. It was the best she could manage. 'And you should think about my suggestion of planting up a hectare or two of Torrington land with Geraldton wax bushes. There's a big demand for it in the florist shops.'

Sam's eyebrows rose. 'I'd forgotten you mentioned that, but it would be a good idea. I'll get right onto it in the new year.'

He stood up and bent to kiss her and Maddy pressed her lips to his smooth cheek in return. Then she took a deep breath to try to hold back the threatening sob. The effort to stop herself from asking about Rick was almost more than she could bear.

Where is he? she pleaded silently.

Clearly unaware of her agitated state, Sam hoisted a small backpack over one shoulder and squeezed Maddy's arm. 'Be seeing you,' he said, and his voice seemed to choke on the words. He walked across the room and out of the door.

She couldn't let him go.

Suddenly it became absolutely vital to Maddy to at least know where Rick was, even though the knowledge would do her no good whatsoever. If he had already left the country, as she had predicted he would, she would know she had lost him. She should put him out of her mind.

For ever.

But, desperate as she was to find out this information,

Maddy stood as if glued to the spot, wanting to run after Sam, but unable to make her feet move. She tried to call his name. 'Sam!' The syllable emerged as no more than a whisper.

Then an explosion of panic sent her flying across the room. She could see him at the end of the hospital corridor. 'Sam!' Again her choked throat could not produce enough volume. A sob of frustration burst from Maddy's lips and with it came the ability to cry out loudly, despairingly. *'Sam!'*

Just in time, Maddy saw the khaki-clad figure halt. Sam turned and squinted back at her. Waving, Maddy hurried down the corridor towards him, but when they met she was almost overcome with another speech impediment.

She gulped.

Sam's dark eyes searched her face, his expression full of deep concern. 'What is it, Maddy?'

'Sam—where—where is he?'

'Don't look so worried,' he cried, and hugged her close. With a callused thumb, Sam stroked a tear from under her eye. 'Rick left this morning for Kuala Lumpur.'

It was as well he was holding her. As she heard Sam's news, Maddy slumped as if her bones had been replaced with sawdust. *Kuala Lumpur!*

'Oh, poppet,' Sam sighed as he helped her to a seat. 'I would have told you, but I wasn't sure if you wanted to know.'

'It's OK.' Maddy rested her head against the wall behind her. 'I was just kind of hoping…'

Sam sat beside her. 'That he'd be hanging around?'

'Yes, I guess so.'

Slinging his backpack onto his knee, Sam unbuckled

a strap. 'Look, I've got something here I was going to leave with you and then I wasn't sure if it was such a bright idea.' He pulled a video tape out of the pack. 'You didn't see the wrap-up of the bushfire reports on last night's TV, did you?'

Maddy shook her head and wondered how on earth Sam could think she would want to look at that now.

Sam placed the tape on her lap. 'My advice is to take a look at it. I'm pretty sure it will make you feel a hell of a lot better.' He stood up and walked across to a water cooler and filled a paper cup. Returning with it to Maddy, he grinned at her. 'If you and that silly mate of mine don't get together soon and get on with what God meant to happen, I'm going to be a grey-haired old man before my time.'

Maddy thanked Sam for the water and took a sip. Her face twisted into a crooked smile. 'If only it were that simple, Sam.'

'Take a look at this anyway.' Sam tapped the video tape with his finger.

The last time Maddy had a tape of a Rick Lawson program, she had thrown it into her rubbish bin. She'd been sorely tempted to do the same thing again just as soon as she returned to her flat, but at the last minute she'd weakened.

But for three days it had sat on her coffee table, untouched.

Watching another program of Rick's would be a form of contact too close for comfort. It was bad enough reliving in her mind, over and over, those last few moments on the hospital balcony when she'd sent him away. Memories of Rick's romantic efforts plagued her. She had no idea how many times she'd read his poem, or played the music box's hauntingly sweet little tune. As for thinking about the meal, the feel and taste of Rick's kisses on the balcony—Maddy doubted that any woman in any time in history had been granted a more beautiful evening.

Why had Rick gone to so much trouble when he knew their situation was hopeless?

He had acknowledged soon after they met that she was a girl who needed more than romance. For Maddy, romance was wonderful, but it was just the fancy trimmings. It was like the icing on the cake without the solid fruity mixture that held the cake together.

The way she felt about Rick, she needed that next drastic step beyond romance—the dreaded *C* word—*commitment*. And Rick had already told her that he couldn't commit. He was afraid of making promises he wouldn't want to keep.

So to look at his face on the screen now, to listen to his voice and watch his mouth curve into a sexy smile would be the worst form of torture. And she'd put herself through enough forms of self-torment this year to last her for another decade.

Last night's news had been bad enough. There had been a segment about the fresh outbreaks of big forest fires in Malaysia and Indonesia and the environmental threats to the people of these countries. When Rick's face had come on the screen, reporting from Kuala Lumpur, she'd wanted to curl up and die.

He'd been wearing an open-necked army-style shirt and he had never looked more handsome as he'd faced the camera, his hair falling softly over one eyebrow as the wind caught it. His actual time on screen had probably lasted no more than thirty seconds. Thirty seconds of bitter agony.

Just half a minute was enough time to reinforce for her the blinding evidence of exactly what she had lost. The man she loved.

This morning, she had given the hardworking Chrissie time off to do some shopping, but as Maddy dragged herself around her shop she knew her eyes were circled by ugly black rings and the rest of her face was red and puffy. Would she ever feel normal again?

With a deep-seated sigh, she set about pricing a row of potted flowering begonias and, despite the remaining bandages, managed to tie pretty ribbons around the pots to entice customers to buy them as gifts.

Even after her luxurious time resting in hospital, she still felt tired. All her energy seemed to be taken up with trying not to care that she would never see Rick again. Every time the phone rang she jumped. There was no chance the caller would be Rick, but never once did she hear that shrill summons without thinking of him. Shortly after lunch, she heard Sam's cheery voice on the end of the line.

'Have you contacted him?'

'Who?'

A loud curse reverberated in Maddy's ear. 'Forgive me, Maddy, but, for crying out loud, I'm talking about Rick of course.'

'Why should I contact him?'

'You haven't looked at it, have you?'

'The video?'

'Yes, the video I gave you in hospital. It shows the last interview with Rick before he left for Malaysia.'

'No, I'm sorry, Sam. I haven't. I—I'd rather not.'

'Give me a break! I'm not used to playing Cupid.' A loud, frustrated sigh came down the line. 'Listen,

Maddy. Can you do me a favour? Look at that damn video. Just as soon as you can. It can't hurt you.'

'Are you sure, Sam? I'm afraid I'm pretty fragile these days.'

There was a long silence on the other end of the phone. When Sam spoke again his voice was very gentle. 'I'd stake my life that it won't hurt you, Maddy.'

'That's certainly a very high wager,' Maddy admitted. She twisted the phone cord with her good hand. 'I—I'll give it a go this afternoon, when Chrissie comes back to the shop.'

When she put the phone down, Maddy began to shake. What on earth could be on this video that was so important?

After last night, she doubted she had the courage to look at more footage of Rick. But Sam had been so insistent and she'd given him her word. Somehow, she filled in the time till Chrissie returned to take over the store. Customers drifted in and out of the shop and she worked on automatic pilot as she attended to them and answered phone calls.

When at last she could slip back into her flat, she rushed straight to the tape and rammed it into the player. Best to get this over with quickly.

Images of the bushfires scrolled across the screen accompanied by the opening music of a popular current affairs program. Impatiently, Maddy watched the first few minutes as the presenter traced the development of the fires, but she found his commentary far too slow. She grabbed the remote control and pressed 'fast forward' until she saw Rick's face flash onto the screen. Her finger jabbed the 'play' button.

He was speaking from a helicopter as it circled above one of the fires.

'Firefighters are struggling to contain this huge bushfire which has already burnt out thousands of hectares of forest and grazing country in the Brisbane valley. The blaze is so intense that it's created a fire storm which is sweeping through the tops of giant gum trees faster than a man can run…'

Just watching the savage, bestial fury of the fire again brought the horror back for Maddy far too vividly. She was about to press 'fast forward', when suddenly there was an image of the normally cool, calm Rick looking white as a sheet with panic. The camera panned past his profile to share his view through the chopper's Perspex window of a fire tanker engulfed in flames.

Oh, Lord, Maddy thought, that was us.

Rick was roaring, 'Cut! For God's sake, cut the camera! This is a tragedy.' His voice cracked with what sounded suspiciously like a sob. 'The woman I love is down there and she might die.'

Startled, Maddy raised a shaking hand to her mouth. It tore at her insides to hear Rick's admission and to see him looking so despairing, so genuinely grief-stricken. She felt her heart lift and then thud painfully. A noisy sob broke from her trembling lips and she missed the next few minutes of the film. It seemed to cut to a later date.

Rick was standing next to a helicopter in front of an expanse of blackened bushland. 'That's right, Jim,' he was saying. 'The next assignment to cover the fires in South-East Asia is to be my last job as a foreign correspondent.'

Maddy froze. Every single nerve-ending in her body seemed to be electrified.

Although the camera remained on Rick, the presenter's questions could be heard in a voice-over coming from the studio. 'This is a shock decision, Rick. You've lived in the teeth of danger for the past decade, taking incredible risks to bring us up-to-the-minute reports from all the world's hot spots. Do you feel you've earned the right to a quiet life? Is that why you're coming home?'

Crouching on the carpet in front of her television set, Maddy chewed at the frayed edge of one of her bandages. She couldn't believe what she was hearing.

'That's not quite the way I look at it, Jim,' Rick replied with his familiar, slow smile. The camera zoomed in on him for a close-up. 'These Australian bushfires and our crew's rescue the other day of a very special lady have reminded me that I have very important responsibilities here in my own country, too. I've realised that it's all very well to be heroic in someone else's territory, but when that can mean putting the lives of those I hold dearly at home in danger it's time to seriously rethink my priorities. I can't think of a better reason for coming home than to demonstrate my commitment to my future family.'

Future family? A strangled sob burst from Maddy's throat.

'I'm sure there are romantic undertones, here,' came the presenter's voice again. 'So we'll look out for news of a Lawson wedding. Is that a distinct possibility, Rick?'

Rick shrugged his broad shoulders and grinned. 'Stranger things have happened.'

'Oh, Rick!' Maddy cried as the picture cut back to the studio and another news segment was introduced. 'Oh, Rick! Oh, sweet heaven.' She pressed 'rewind' and she played the segment through again, just to make sure she wasn't mistaken.

Rick was giving up his foreign fieldwork. He wanted

to come home to Australia to start a family. What had she done? Rick had tried to tell her he loved her. He'd even gone to considerable lengths to fulfil her romantic dreams. And she had coldly dismissed him. She hadn't given him a chance to explain.

After their wonderful dinner, she'd waltzed back to her room like a haughty queen who'd been displeased with the best efforts of a lowly servant.

When he'd tried to explain, she hadn't been prepared to listen. She hadn't trusted him!

Oh, Lord! Maddy paced around the room frantically, unable to think clearly. But at last one coherent thought filtered through. She had to tell Rick she was sorry and that she loved him, needed him, couldn't face another day without him.

She couldn't possibly wait till he returned from Malaysia. Maddy dashed to the telephone book and flipped frantically through the pages till she found the number of an international airline. Then, as she began to punch in the numbers, a happy sigh escaped her. She was starting to feel better already.

CHAPTER ELEVEN

AND fate was on her side for once.

There was a late cancellation and a seat was available on the late afternoon flight to Malaysia. After making more arrangements with the long-suffering Chrissie about looking after the shop, Maddy dashed around her flat, throwing clothes into an overnight bag in an excited flurry.

By the time she reached the departure lounge at the Brisbane International terminal, Maddy was quite worked up. She sat stiffly on the edge of her chair and checked her ticket and her passport for the tenth time. It wasn't at all like her to be fidgety over minor practical details, but she was so desperate to see Rick again that she found she was worrying about everything. Was she at the correct exit gate? Was her flight number right? Luckily, because she'd only thrown a few items together into the overnight bag, she'd been able to keep it as hand luggage, so at least she didn't have to worry about whether her baggage was loaded onto the correct plane.

She tried to calm herself by thinking about Rick's reaction when she turned up at his hotel. Sam had been so excited when she'd rung to check where Rick would be staying. As he'd told her the name of the hotel chain the network used, he'd hardly been able to contain his glee.

'Go for it, kiddo!' he'd cheered when he heard her plans. 'Yes! Just run into his arms and do all that movie type stuff. Oh, boy! I'm so relieved.'

The phone call to her mother had been quite a different experience.

'Malaysia? But, Maddy, whatever for?'

'I want to visit a friend there.'

'But, darling, you're just out of hospital, for heaven's sake. This is the last thing you should be doing. I thought you were coming here. You know I wanted you to come home as soon as you were discharged. And it's your father's birthday tomorrow.'

'Mum, I'm really sorry about missing Dad's birthday, but this is very important to me. I'm feeling fine. Wonderful in fact.'

Perhaps she had sounded just a little too happy, Maddy reflected now. Her mother's voice had changed from distressed to suspicious. 'This wouldn't have anything to do with that hearts-and-flowers mail you received in hospital, would it?'

Maddy had grimaced. 'Yes and no.'

There had been a longish silence on the other end of the line. 'I presume this is all about a man. Are we going to be told anything about him?'

Maddy hesitated. It was on the tip of her tongue to tell her mother everything about Rick. Especially how very, very much she loved him, but it had hardly seemed fair to tell her mother when she hadn't even told Rick. 'I'll bring him to meet you just as soon as I can.'

'So you're quite sure racing off like this is wise?'

'Yes, Mum. Please, don't worry about me. I'll keep in touch and I'll be home again very soon.'

Now, Maddy wondered how she could possibly sit patiently on an aeroplane for several more hours before she saw Rick again. She desperately needed to feel his arms around her once more. She wanted him so badly it hurt. Once again, she checked her watch against the times listed on the display board. In five minutes, her flight should be boarding...

She felt better once her seat belt was secured and all the passengers were settled. Any minute now the plane would take off and there was nothing to stop her being with Rick. During the flight, she would listen to some light music, watch a video, eat a meal...and in no time at all she would be in Rick's arms.

She opened a magazine and tried to will herself to relax. But she was distracted when a woman in an official uniform appeared at the cabin door and began to talk earnestly to one of the flight attendants. Maddy felt a twinge of alarm. Surely there wasn't gong to be some little drama to hold them up? Her stomach fluttered nervously as the attendant frowned and cast a baleful eye over the seated passengers. It certainly looked as if something was wrong.

Maddy surveyed the cabin full of people. It was a very normal collection of passengers. She wondered what could be the problem.

When her eyes swung back to the flight attendant at the front of the plane, she realised to her horror that the woman was staring at her. The attendant made definite eye contact with Maddy and then headed straight down the aisle towards her. Her stomach clenched and she felt quite ill.

'Ms Delancy?'

'Yes?' Maddy's sweating hands gripped the arms of her seat.

'There's a gentleman outside who claims to have an urgent message for you.'

'A what? Who?' Maddy's heart was pounding in her throat. 'Is something wrong?'

'Could you come this way, please?'

'No, I'm sorry. I can't leave the plane. It's very important that I get to Kuala Lumpur tonight.' Maddy struggled to make sense of this nightmare.

The flight attendant offered her most placating smile. 'There's no suggestion that you won't be able to re-board this flight as soon as you've spoken to the messenger,' she said.

Maddy scrambled reluctantly out of her seat. 'It's not my family, is it? Nothing's happened to my parents?'

'I don't think so.' The flight attendant tried to reassure her. 'Someone from our ground staff here will explain. Is this your bag? I'll bring it for you.'

At the main cabin exit, a bright-eyed woman greeted her. 'Ms Delancy?'

'Yes,' Maddy repeated weakly.

'Could you come this way, please?'

'I have to leave the plane?' Clutching her bag tightly to her chest, Maddy stared at the woman in dismay. All she could think of was the lovely reunion with Rick she had planned in Kuala Lumpur. Surely now, at the very last minute, fate wasn't going to work against her?

'It's just for a few moments.'

'Well—will I be allowed back on this plane?'

'If you still want to take the flight.'

If I still want to? Oh, Lord, thought Maddy wretchedly. *Something really terrible must have happened.* She wondered how her trembling legs would hold her up as she followed the woman away from the plane.

They reached the electronically controlled glass doors that opened back into the departure lounge. There was a man standing there, his hands thrust in his pockets and his expression grim.

Stunned, Maddy felt the colour rush from her face.

Her legs were trembling. There was no way she could move.

'Rick?'

'Hi, Maddy.'

He looked so wonderful, she felt her heart jump in her chest. 'What on earth are you dong here?'

'Looking for you.' Rick stood quite still as if he was frozen to the spot.

'Why didn't you tell me you were coming home?'

His mouth twisted into a shy smile. 'I thought I had more chance of sweeping you off your feet this way.'

'I—I thought you were—I thought something had happened to my family— Oh, Rick, it's so good to see you.' She stepped tentatively towards him, smiling through her tears. 'How did you find me?'

'With great difficulty.'

Rick seemed different. He was normally so relaxed, so in charge of any situation, but now he looked extremely tense. 'How are you?' she asked softly.

'I'm fine now I'm looking at you,' he whispered back. He wiped a sleeve across his eyes and Maddy's throat contracted over a huge knot of emotion. 'How are you, Maddy? How are your hands?'

She managed a shaky smile and held her lightly bandaged hands out for his inspection. 'It's amazing, really, how quickly skin can heal. It will be a while before the right one is completely back to normal. But it doesn't bother me at all.'

Rick nodded. 'That's great.' But he was still looking dreadfully agitated.

She scolded him gently. 'You look like a soldier standing to attention. All solemn and stiff and formal.'

'That's because I'm so damn scared, Maddy. I've

faced despots, criminals and stray bullets with ten times more poise than this.'

She wanted to throw her arms around him, to reassure him, but his uncertainty held her back. Maddy tried a different tack. 'I was going to Malaysia to find you,' she said.

'Chrissie told me.' He smiled. 'I couldn't believe it after the fuss I kicked up in Kuala Lumpur to be allowed back to Australia today. But after I spoke to Chrissie I told myself that you must have decided you wanted to be with me. I decided there was no way you would travel so far just to tell me to get lost.'

'I had a very different message in mind,' she told him, and a happy thrill raced through her when she saw his face relax. 'When did you get back?'

'About an hour ago,' he said. 'I got to the shop and then got the news that you'd already left. I've been racing like the blazes to catch you before take-off. I had to pull every trick in the book to get you off that plane.'

They stood staring at each other, both a little shy, both aware they were on the edge of a very significant moment. Neither wanting to get it wrong.

'What did you tell them?' she asked, trying to relax her face, to smile at him. It seemed to be impossible.

'That the woman I love was on that plane. That I wanted to ask her to marry me.'

'And—and they believed you?'

He stood staring at her, his eyes glittering and his mouth a nervous, tight line.

Her heart in her mouth, Maddy stepped tentatively towards him. 'Rick, I think this is where you're supposed to sweep me into your arms and kiss me—passionately.'

His smile broke through then and he lifted trembling

hands to her face. 'That would be the romantic thing to do, wouldn't it?'

She nodded and bit her lip.

'But I tried romance, Maddy, and I botched it. I want to get things right this time.'

'Oh, Rick,' Maddy cried, 'you never did get the romance wrong. I was being silly. I was frightened of trusting another man hot on the heels of my experience with Byron. When you said you loved me, I just couldn't bring myself to believe it.'

He smiled a careful smile. 'But you believe me now? You think I should have another crack at romance?'

'You don't need to, Rick. You got it right the first time.' She lifted her face to his, her expression suddenly earnest. 'I saw the interview on television—what you said about giving up your job. Are you sure you won't miss it?'

For answer, he drew her face up to his and brushed his lips against hers. Then her mouth opened like a flower under his and he deepened the kiss. Her arms wound around his neck and her curves leaned into his strength.

'Ah, Maddy,' he sighed. 'It will be a minor miracle if I keep this respectable. We are, after all, in a public place.'

A cough behind them caught his attention. The airline employee had approached. Her eyes were red and she was blowing her nose fiercely. 'This plane has to leave. Did you want to return to your seat?' she asked Maddy.

'Oh, no, thank you.'

The woman began to snuffle into a tissue again as she hurried back to the intercom. 'Good luck, you guys,' she called.

Rick waved to her. 'Thanks for your help.' To Maddy, he said, 'Do you mind being proposed to in an airport?'

'Proposed to? Have I missed something?'

Rick frowned. 'I thought I told you I want to marry you.'

'You told the airline people, not me.'

He trailed a finger across her lips and took a deep breath. 'Madeline Delancy, I love you and—and I want to share the rest of my life with you. Every day—not just snatches of time here and there. Will you marry me?'

She touched his cheek. 'Oh, Rick, I can't bear the thought of not being married to you.' Her eyes swept the empty departure lounge. 'And I can't think of any place better for a proposal.'

Soon a new group of travellers would start to fill this space again, but for a brief moment it had been theirs. Serviceable deep blue carpet, rows of deep blue and green upholstered seats, the odd pot plant. It was entirely ordinary, but she wanted to imprint it on her mind.

'Let's get moving,' murmured Rick. He slung her carry bag over one shoulder.

Happily, Maddy walked beside him, with her arm linked through his. She almost felt on top of the world, but there was still something bothering her. 'Rick, I really need to know that you are OK about giving up the foreign fieldwork. Will you really be happy just covering national news?'

He dropped a light kiss on her brow. 'If I'm honest, there are sure to be the odd occasions when I will miss some parts of that job. But I'm fooling myself really if I think that news happening here can't be just as significant as news from anywhere else. Besides, I know damn well that if I stay overseas I will miss a whole pile of more important things.'

'For example?' Maddy asked cautiously, her heartbeat accelerating.

'Example number one—I can't bear being away from you any more, Maddy.'

'You're quite sure?'

He stopped, swept her up and spun her around, before planting a resounding kiss on her laughing mouth. There was a smattering of applause from some travellers in a nearby coffee shop. 'I'm quite sure, my sweet girl. I had a taste of life overseas without you in Hong Kong and I was miserable enough then, but this last trip to Malaysia has been pure hell. I nearly got myself sacked. I couldn't concentrate on the job. Kept thinking about you all the damn time.' He tucked her arm back through his and they continued walking. 'And I don't want to miss out on all the chicken cacciatore meals or the marinated beef strips. I love the fact that you're such a little homemaker, Maddy. And I don't want to miss all the little milestones, either.'

'Milestones?'

'Yes, you know—baby's first smile, the first tooth, first steps—that sort of thing.'

'Babies? Rick, are you sure you want babies?'

'Dozens of them.'

Maddy laughed. 'I don't know if I'm up to that.'

He grinned and kissed the tip of her nose. 'If you'd prefer, we can have them one or two at a time and just see how we take to parenting.'

'I'm sure you'll be all-round amazing,' Maddy murmured.

Rick grinned again. 'I can see that will be my next assignment.'

Maddy looked at him with a perplexed frown. 'Please explain.'

He dazzled her with his most sexy grin to date. 'What a chore—having to sire all those infants.'

She thumped him playfully with her good hand.

At the top of the escalators, they paused in front of a row of shops. In the window of one, a young woman was dressing a dummy. Rick laughed. 'Shop windows have a whole new meaning for me.'

Puzzled again, Maddy surveyed the windows, trying to see which one was so interesting. 'What do you mean?'

'That's how we met,' he said, pointing to the woman busily pulling an outback jacket into place on a mannequin. 'That's how I ended up in your shop. I was attracted to your cute behind in your shop window before I even saw your stunning smile. I had absolutely no intention of buying blue irises or any other kind of flowers that day. But I thought you were about to tumble off that ladder and I had great plans to rescue you.'

Maddy laughed and looked up at him, her eyes dancing with delight. 'Prince Valiant right from the start.' Her expression grew more serious. 'Honestly, Rick, I do value that about you—the way you seem to know me and understand me so well. I do appreciate everything you've done for me. You make me feel so protected.'

They reached the escalators and shared a step as it took them to the ground floor. Rick's arms rested possessively around Maddy's shoulders and she felt so happy, she thought she might literally burst. This really is happening, she kept telling herself as she looked around at the busy airport, trying to convince herself that she wasn't dreaming. Nearby, she saw an excited group of people welcoming a family member home.

'I need to ring my mother to warn her I'll be bringing you home a little earlier than I thought, Rick. You will come out to the farm and meet them all, won't you? It's my father's birthday tomorrow. You can be his present.'

'I won't be too much of a shock to your family?'

'Of course you will, but they'll cope.' Maddy favoured him with a reassuring kiss before hurrying to a pay-phone.

Rick stood close by as she made the call and it was with relief that she turned to him minutes later. 'Mum's ecstatic. I've never heard her sound so excited. And Dad will be, too, when he hears the news. I don't think I've ever told you, but my father is one of your biggest fans.'

Arms linked, they headed towards the taxi rank beyond the terminal's huge glass doors. Maddy was bubbling.

Suddenly Rick halted, his movement so abrupt, Maddy almost tripped. 'I almost forgot something.' He reached into his pocket and drew out a small velvet box.

Her eyes widened as he flipped it open and took her hand in his. 'It's lucky your left hand is so much better,' he murmured. 'It means your ring finger is ready for action.' He slipped a glittering solitaire diamond ring onto her finger, then kissed her. 'I was determined to win you this time, Maddy, so I came prepared.'

'It's so beautiful.'

Ignoring the people rushing busily around them, he kissed her again. 'Will you be my live-in lover?' he asked her.

'Most definitely,' she answered, her eyes brimming with happiness.

'No pretending?'

Maddy blinked back tears. 'I never pretended to love you, Rick. I think it was always the real thing.'

Rick smiled and nodded. 'We're on permanent loan to each other now. Correct?'

'For ever,' she promised.

'That should be just long enough.'

MILLS & BOON

Makes any time special

Enjoy a romantic novel from
Mills & Boon®

Presents...   *Enchanted*™   TEMPTATION.

Historical Romance™   MEDICAL ROMANCE

Hiring Ms. Right

Three single women, one home-help agency—and three professional bachelors in search of...a wife?

- ✯ Are you a busy executive with a demanding career?
- ✯ Do you need help with those time-consuming everyday errands?
- ✯ Ever wished you could hire a house-sitter, caterer...or even a glamorous partner for that special social occasion?

Meet **Cassie**, **Sabrina** and **Paige**—three independent women who've formed a business taking care of those troublesome domestic crises.

And meet the three gorgeous bachelors who are simply looking for a little help...and instead discover they've hired Ms Right!

Enjoy bestselling author **Leigh Michaels's** new trilogy:

HUSBAND ON DEMAND—March 2000
BRIDE ON LOAN—May 2000
WIFE ON APPROVAL—July 2000

Enchanted™

COMING NEXT MONTH

MILLS & BOON®
Enchanted™

THE OUTBACK AFFAIR by Elizabeth Duke

Natasha was horrified when her tour guide turned out to be Tom Scanlon—the man who'd once jilted her. It was too intimate a situation for ex-lovers—but Tom wanted Natasha back. And now he had two weeks alone with her to prove just how much!

THE BEST MAN AND THE BRIDESMAID
by Liz Fielding

As chief bridesmaid, Daisy is forced out of her usual shapeless garb and into a beautiful dress. Suddenly the best man, determinedly single Robert Furneval, whom she has always loved, begins to see her in a whole new light...

HUSBAND ON DEMAND by Leigh Michaels

Jake Abbott has arrived at his brother's house—to discover that Cassie has been hired to look after the residence. He's clearly very happy for their temporary living arrangements to become more intimate. But what about permanent...?

THE FEISTY FIANCÉE by Jessica Steele

When Yanice fell for her boss, Thomson Wakefield, she adhered to her belief that love means marriage, but did it mean the same for him? A near tragic accident brings her answer, but can Yanice trust the proposal of a man under heavy sedation?

Available from 3rd March 2000

Available at most branches of WH Smith, Tesco, Martins, Borders, Easons, Volume One/James Thin and most good paperback bookshops

For the incurable romantic

MILLS & BOON®

Enchanted™

Warm and tender novels that let you experience the magic of falling in love.

Eight brand new titles each month.

Available at most branches of WH Smith, Tesco, Martins, Borders, Easons, Volume One/James Thin and most good paperback bookshops

MILLS & BOON®

By Request™

Three bestselling romances brought back to you by popular demand

Latin Lovers

The Heat of Passion by *Lynne Graham*
Carlo vowed to bring Jessica to her knees, however much she rejected him. But now she faced a choice: three months in Carlo's bed, or her father would go to jail.

The Right Choice by *Catherine George*
When Georgia arrived in Italy to teach English to little Alessa, she was unprepared for her uncle, the devastating Luca. Could she resist?

Vengeful Seduction by *Cathy Williams*
Lorenzo wanted revenge. Isobel had betrayed him once—now she had to pay. But the tears and pain of sacrifice had been price enough. Now she wanted to win him back.

Available at branches of WH Smith, Tesco, Martins, Borders, Easons, Volume One/James Thin and most good paperback bookshops

FREE!

2 Books
and a surprise gift!

We would like to take this opportunity to thank you for reading this Mills & Boon® book by offering you the chance to take TWO more specially selected titles from the Enchanted™ series absolutely FREE! We're also making this offer to introduce you to the benefits of the Reader Service™ —

- ★ FREE home delivery
- ★ FREE gifts and competitions
- ★ FREE monthly Newsletter
- ★ Books available before they're in the shops
- ★ Exclusive Reader Service discounts

Accepting these FREE books and gift places you under no obligation to buy; you may cancel at any time, even after receiving your free shipment. Simply complete your details below and return the entire page to the address below. **You don't even need a stamp!**

YES! Please send me 2 free Enchanted books and a surprise gift. I understand that unless you hear from me, I will receive 4 superb new titles every month for just £2.40 each, postage and packing free. I am under no obligation to purchase any books and may cancel my subscription at any time. The free books and gift will be mine to keep in any case.

NOEB

Ms/Mrs/Miss/Mr ....Initials................................

BLOCK CAPITALS PLEASE

Surname...

Address..

....

....Postcode ....

Send this whole page to:
UK: The Reader Service, FREEPOST CN81, Croydon, CR9 3WZ
EIRE: The Reader Service, PO Box 4546, Kilcock, County Kildare (stamp required)

Offer not valid to current Reader Service subscribers to this series. We reserve the right to refuse an application and applicants must be aged 18 years or over. Only one application per household. Terms and prices subject to change without notice. Offer expires 31st August 2000. As a result of this application, you may receive further offers from Harlequin Mills & Boon Limited and other carefully selected companies. If you would prefer not to share in this opportunity please write to The Data Manager at the address above.

Mills & Boon is a registered trademark owned by Harlequin Mills & Boon Limited.
Enchanted is being used as a trademark.

MILLS & BOON®

Makes Mother's Day special

For Mother's Day this year, why not spoil yourself with a gift from Mills & Boon®.

Enjoy three romance novels by three of your favourite authors and a FREE silver effect picture frame for only £6.99.

Pack includes:

Presents...™
One Night With His Wife by Lynne Graham

Enchanted™
The Faithful Bride by Rebecca Winters

TEMPTATION.
Everything About Him by Rita Clay Estrada

Available from 18th February